The vehicle followed, <!-- obscured --> name—her real name. No bullet for her. Just a hit and run with her own car. A greasy spot on the pavement.

She wasn't about to let them win that easily. As she ran, her hand dived inside her pack and closed around the handle of a 10mm Glock pistol.

"Maddie!" The male voice called again. Too familiar. And impossible!

Her racing feet jerked to a halt, and she pivoted on her heel, Glock extended in both hands. The Oldsmobile's tires locked, and the car skidded toward her. The scent of burnt rubber met Maddie's nostrils as she leaped up and forward. The vehicle rocked to a halt, bumper covering the spot where she'd been standing. She landed atop the hood on her knees and the knuckles of one fist. The other arm trained the Glock on the driver.

He lifted his hands, palms out, lips pressed into a tight line.

Blood pounded in Maddie's ears and blackness edged her vision. It *was* him.

The most gorgeous man on the planet. He was supposed to be dead, but he was alive.

She should shoot him.

Books by Jill Elizabeth Nelson

Love Inspired Suspense

Evidence of Murder
Witness to Murder
Calculated Revenge
Legacy of Lies
Betrayal on the Border

JILL ELIZABETH NELSON

writes what she likes to read—faith-based tales of adventure seasoned with romance. By day she operates as housing manager for a seniors' apartment complex. By night she turns into a wild and crazy writer who can hardly wait to jot down all the exciting things her characters are telling her, so she can share them with her readers. More about Jill and her books can be found at www.jillelizabethnelson.com. She and her husband live in rural Minnesota, surrounded by the woods and prairie and their four grown children who have settled nearby.

JILL ELIZABETH NELSON

Betrayal
on the Border

Love Inspired

Recycling programs
for this product may
not exist in your area.

™ LOVE INSPIRED BOOKS

ISBN-13: 978-0-373-44516-5

BETRAYAL ON THE BORDER

www.LoveInspiredBooks.com

Printed in U.S.A.

He that dwelleth in the secret place of the most High shall abide under the shadow of the Almighty. I will say of the Lord, He is my refuge and my fortress: my God; in him will I trust.... A thousand shall fall at thy side, and ten thousand at thy right hand; but it shall not come nigh thee. Only with thine eyes shalt thou behold and see the reward of the wicked.

—*Psalm* 91:1–2, 7–8

To the brave, honest and loyal men and women who protect and serve on the front lines of the war on drugs. May you dwell securely under the shadow of the Almighty and walk in supernatural triumph as you battle with spiritual weapons greater than what is common to man.

ONE

If that off-white chunk of clay was craftsman's putty, Maddie Jameson would eat her tool belt. What was C-4 explosive compound doing on the kitchen table in this unit at Morningside Apartments? A chill rippled her insides.

Not everyone would recognize the remnants from the construction of a pipe bomb. To the untrained eye, the dab of C-4 could be mistaken for putty and the bits of wire and lengths of sawed-off pipe merely scraps from a handyman project. But then, not many apartment-maintenance workers were ex–army rangers with Maddie's skill set— or a history that meant she must keep her head down and her eyes peeled.

Those who hunted her were relentless and ruthless, and she was damaged prey. She needed to see them coming before they got to her.

Not that she ever knew exactly what hired assassin would be after her. She could bump into one on the street and not know it until he tried to take her out. Everyone was a suspect. If only she could figure out why she was marked for death. Had she seen something the night of the attack a year ago on the Rio Grande? If so, her head injury had erased it from her memory.

Was she the target of the bomb these Morningside tenants had been making? If the three attempts on her life within the past year were any clue, she'd be an idiot to think otherwise. Where was the bomb planted? Her care-taker's apartment on the premises? Maddie's mouth went dry. There could be collateral damage. Dozens of people—including children—lived in this building, and a bomb didn't care who it destroyed.

Dear God, please don't let innocent families be hurt because of me.

Fighting for a full breath, she looked down at the work order in her hand. No, she hadn't made a mistake. The order listed this apartment and stated that the tenants had given permission for the maintenance person to enter in their absence in order to replace a torn window screen. But she'd checked the screens—they were whole. Why would the tenants give permission for her to enter the premises on a trumped-up excuse and then leave their bomb-making scraps lying around in plain view?

Unless this was a trap.

The air in Maddie's lungs went arctic. Maybe the bomb was planted in this very unit. The timer could click down to zero at any second.

Her feet cried *Run—seek safety somewhere...anywhere!* But flight wouldn't help the other people who could be blown to smithereens.

Sweat trickled down her scalp, despite the coolness blowing from the wall-mounted air conditioner. The scar above her right ear itched, but she ignored the sensation as she yanked her two-way radio from her belt and began to search the premises with her eyes. There wasn't much space to cover in this studio apartment. A kitchenette. A living-room area with an easy chair and matching ottoman, a television the tenants had left blaring, and a couch that had been slept on, if the rumpled bedding was any indication. A hide-a-bed pulled out from the wall filled the rest of the space. That, too, hosted a nest of wadded bedding.

"Bill, do you have a copy?" Maddie spoke into the radio.

She took her thumb off the button and listened for a response. Silence answered. *Great!* The apartment manager had chosen this critical moment to be absent from his office.

Maddie gingerly cracked the oven door open and peered inside. No bomb. She checked the refrigerator. A half-gallon carton of milk, a partially eaten brick of cheese and an overripe peach, but no bomb. She opened the cupboards with one hand while using the other to keep calling for Bill every few seconds. Still no answer. Her throat tensed as if invisible fingers had tightened around her windpipe. A little voice in her head screamed she was running out of time.

The tenants in this unit had opted not to hook up a landline phone, and company regulations dictated that employees not carry cell phones. Bad policy in this instance. Maybe she should run to the office herself and phone for the bomb squad. But the bomb could go off in her absence and kill any of the neighbors above, below or on either side. If she found the apparatus, she could defuse it as well as— or better than—the police experts.

She went to the clothes closet and pulled back the sliding door. *Phew!* The scent of onions rolled out. One of the owners of the stack of luggage that filled most of the space must have a love affair with the vegetable she most despised. Maddie let out a heavy sigh. She'd have to search each bag, and she'd be surprised if she didn't find a different name on every airline tag. Crooks who wanted to fly under the system's radar sometimes generated pocket money by walking off with pieces from baggage carousels and pawning or selling the contents.

From the hallway came the sound of male voices. They

drew nearer…nearer…and then stopped on the other side of the apartment entrance. Maddie froze. The tenants were returning? Then the bomb wasn't here. Her shoulders slumped, but then her gut tensed. It was too late to slip away unseen. She could hide in the closet with the onion odor, but to what purpose? If the tenants were in for the evening, she'd be found eventually. There was no way to exit this third-floor unit except through the front door.

Well, then, that's how she'd leave. If she could bluff her way out, fine. If not… Tingles traveled down her extremities. Her muscles gathered. Combat instincts reared their ugly heads. Instincts she wished to forget. Instincts she might need. Again.

Maddie clipped the radio onto her belt and shoved the closet door shut as a click sounded in the entrance lock. A pair of men stepped inside, closed the door and then halted at the sight of her. Above a tall, whipcord body, a dark face with reddened eyes glared at her, lips peeled back from white teeth. Behind him, a short, pale man with doughy cheeks gaped in an astonished O.

She forced a smile and held out her work order. "I was sent to repair your screen, but I can't find any damage."

Lanky Man's face grew darker as a spark of recognition lit his ink-black eyes. She didn't know him, but he knew her. How? His hand slid beneath the front of his suit jacket as Dough Man leaped toward the table.

With a feral growl, Maddie dropped the work-order slip and swept her leg toward Lanky Man—her immediate threat. Her heel hooked the back of his knee. *Crack!* A handgun discharged while her assailant toppled backward. The bullet pinged against metal—likely a piece of the sprinkler system.

Cursing, threat number two rushed toward her, length of pipe raised. She chopped the rigid edge of her left hand into the soft bend of his elbow. The pipe fell from the arm she had numbed, and her right-handed chop connected with his Adam's apple. The man went down, gagging and clutching his throat.

She whirled toward threat number one, who was climbing to his feet and bringing his Beretta to bear. Her radio squawked as her leg swept up, higher this time, and the heel of her work boot struck the smaller bone near the gunman's wrist. The bone broke with an audible snap, and the gun rocketed into the far wall. Roaring and cradling his disabled hand, Lanky Man charged her, shoulder in ramming position.

Maddie danced aside, but the calf of her leg met the ottoman. She lost the fight for balance and tumbled backward onto the soft body of the Dough Man. Air gushed from his chest, and the struggle to breathe through his damaged windpipe faded into limpness beneath her. Her radio squawked again with Bill's voice calling for her.

Now *he wanted to talk? Sorry, pal, I'm a little busy!*

The toe of a hard shoe hammered Maddie's side. Pain splintered through her, and a scream rent her throat even as she rolled away from the next kick. From a catlike crouch, she caught the foot intended for her face and sprang upward while twisting her assailant's ankle into an unnatural position. Lanky Man howled as his other foot left the floor. Airborne, he flipped and dropped, face-first, onto the unforgiving floor. Stunned and groaning, he lay still.

Maddie scooped up the gun and held it on her attackers, then pulled her radio from her belt.

"Bill, do you have a copy?"

"Maddie, where are you?" *Static.* "I've been trying to raise you to let you know the wrong apartment number was entered on the work order. The damaged screen is in Apartment 312, not 315."

"Copy that, Bill, but there's been an incident in Apartment 315. Call the police and the paramedics. And tell them to send the bomb squad. We need to evac this building."

Heartbeats of radio silence were punctuated by another moan from the floor. The lean one stirred.

"Are you serious?" Bill's voice came over the air in a tight squeak.

"Do it *now*." A grim smile lifted her lips. About time she had the opportunity to order the paper-pusher around.

Lanky Man eased to a sitting position, glaring at her above a bloodied nose. The pale one lay inert. His throat was swollen, but his chest moved up and down. She had refrained from striking with deadly force. There was a time when that wouldn't have been the case.

A time when she didn't live like a hunted creature, scurrying from burrow to burrow. Thanks to these two scum of the earth, it was time to run again. But first—

"Where's the bomb?" She extended the gun toward her conscious assailant.

He curled a swollen lip.

"You can tell me, or you can tell the cops. Or maybe the FBI. Someone like you is probably on their list."

The alarm began to blare in the hallway, summoning the residents to evacuate, but Lanky Man's gaze darted toward the television set. Maddie followed his stare, and her jaw dropped. The camera zoomed in on the flaming wreckage of a midsize sedan sitting at the end of a row of vehicles in a large lot. Maddie strained her ears to hear the commentator above the scream of the alarm.

"Thirty minutes ago, a bomb exploded in a car outside San Antonio's Embassy Suites Airport Hotel." The female news anchor spoke with a practiced air of concern.

Maddie's heart rate stalled and then raced. Unless these zeros had made *two* bombs, she wasn't the target. That meant a pair of vital things—the innocent residents at Morningside were likely safe, but someone else had already died. Who?

"The Chevrolet Impala was rented yesterday by this man," the newscaster went on.

The report cut to a grainy security-camera shot of a tall, broad-shouldered figure dressed in a sport shirt and slacks, standing at the Enterprise rental counter of the San Antonio International Airport. The face was blurred, but Maddie's grip loosened around the butt of the Beretta.

No! She couldn't be seeing right.

Then a professional head shot of the same dynamic, thirtysomething man filled the 42-inch screen. Larger than life, he grinned at her with perfect teeth. An aquiline nose, tanned complexion and artfully tousled brown hair shouted class and hinted at arrogance. The glint in his eyes and the square of his chin spoke equal parts daring and determination.

A squeak left Maddie's throat. Lanky Man made a sudden movement, but she leaped back and cocked the gun. He raised his hands in surrender and went still as the newscaster continued speaking words that hammered in Maddie's brain.

"Christopher David Mason, an Emmy Award-winning reporter for *World News,* is presumed dead in the blast. The authorities have not yet been able to approach the vehicle to recover the remains. Mason is best known for his award-winning coverage of the massacre along the Rio Grande that occurred one year ago last month. The tragedy claimed the lives of all but himself and one member of an international team of military and law enforcement personnel. The team was scheduled the next day to mount an assault on the main stronghold of the Ortiz drug cartel near Nuevo Laredo, Mexico."

As the woman eulogized, the vivid blue of Chris's eyes gripped Maddie, ensnared her. She tumbled into them, helpless. He'd always had that affect on her. To her shame. Guilt twisted her gut. How could she be attracted to a traitor! Someone on the ground with them that night on the Rio had to have betrayed their location to the cartel forces they were supposed to take out the next morning. She knew she didn't betray her team, so it had to have been Chris. He belonged behind bars. Suffering. Anywhere but in the grave like the others.

"The Ortiz Cartel claimed responsibility for the Rio Grande Massacre," the newscaster continued. "Today's fresh tragedy begs the question—have they struck again? And, if so, why? We hope to have more information for our viewers on the late news."

The program switched to the weather. Hot. Sunny. No rain in sight. Nothing unusual in that forecast for mid-June in Texas, but her world had just turned inside out one more time.

An hour later, the bomb squad had searched the building and declared all clear. The tenants were released to return to their dwellings, while the tight-lipped suspects were hustled off to jail. Maddie strode toward her first-floor corner apartment.

The cops had been tickled to gain custody of the bombers so quickly after the explosion in the hotel parking lot. It was easy to secure their promise to keep Maddie's involvement in the arrest confidential. Her reprieve from further scrutiny would be temporary, however. The police had taken her fingerprints for elimination on the gun. When they ran the prints, hopefully not too soon, they'd sit up and take notice that Madison Jameson was really Madeleine Jerrard, former communications specialist with the army ranger unit slaughtered in the Rio Grande Massacre. The link to the freshly murdered Chris Mason would be obvious, and they'd look to bring her in for further questioning, but they wouldn't find her. Neither would those who wanted her dead.

Maddie reached her apartment, glanced up and down the empty hallway, then slipped inside and shut the door. Normally, this would be the moment in her day when she would strip the band from her ponytail, shake her thick, dusty-blond hair loose around her shoulders and head to the bathroom for a good, long soak in a tub of scented water. Not this evening.

Her head injuries had stolen critical memories of that night along the Rio Grande, but the cartel—or more likely an official in their pocket on *this* side of the river—thought she'd seen something that would expose them. She'd been on the run since their first attempt on her life barely a week after her release from the military hospital.

Too bad her faceless mortal enemy didn't know she couldn't remember whatever it was that might incriminate him. He might not be so set on doing her in then. Of course, a traitor to his country had motive to be hyper-paranoid. He'd probably sign her death warrant regardless, on the off chance that she *might* remember.

Now they'd tied up another of their other loose ends by taking out one of their accomplices in the very city where she hid, which meant Chris had probably been on the hunt for her and closing in. His killers had recently rented an apartment where she worked and lived. No coincidence there. Her enemies had located her, and their hired goons had intended her to be their next target...if she hadn't stumbled onto them first through a mix-up in apartment numbers.

Random providence? Or the hand of the God she doubted?

She didn't have time to seek answers to a spiritual question. As soon as her faceless enemy discovered their boys had been nabbed, they'd maneuver fresh troops into place to finish the job. Maddie's heart rate slowed, her breathing deepened and her senses sharpened. Even the hum of the refrigerator motor sounded loud in her ears. She'd been in this position before and knew what to do.

She swift-footed to the bedroom, shedding her tool belt on the way and letting it thump to the carpet. In less than a minute, she had removed her jeans, work boots and button-down shirt that made her look like a skinny tomboy and donned a pair of casual capris, pullover top and running shoes with tennis socks that gave her the appearance of any other lean, mean soccer mom in this middle-class neighborhood. Not that she was a mom. Never yet had that chance in her twenty-eight years of life.

From the bread-loaf-size purse on the dresser, she removed all the cash, then went to the closet and tugged a string that looked like it went to a lightbulb but didn't. A hatch she'd made in the ceiling popped open and dropped a bulging backpack. She caught it, then headed for the bathroom, where she tossed into the pack the emergency makeup kit she kept ready for this moment.

The mirror over the sink betrayed the tension sharpening her rather angular features. Chris was dead? The shock left a vacant cavity in the pit of her stomach. She truly was the only survivor from the massacre on the Rio—but for how long? Tears attempted to pool in the corners of her eyes. She pressed the heels of her palms against her cheekbones then splashed cold water on her face.

Grief would have to wait—like it always did.

Maddie turned on her heel and left the apartment, senses alert for threat.

Two hours later, she descended from the bowels of a metro bus in an industrial district. The bus pulled out with a hiss of air brakes and a spurt of diesel fumes, leaving her standing on the sidewalk.

Her gaze consumed her surroundings. Pedestrians' activities raised no red flags. The spotty after-hours traffic behaved normally. Everyone seemed to be minding their own business.

Excellent!

She'd spent the past hours switching buses at random until she was reasonably convinced no one followed. The imaginary bull's-eye between her shoulder blades itched nonetheless. She shrugged her shoulders against the weight of her pack and stepped into the crosswalk. Gathering dusk spread long shadows. Maddie followed hers across the street and into the ground-floor bay of a long-term parking garage.

The *pad-pad* of her running shoes echoed faintly in the cavernous space. Her gaze searched the dimness as she trod to the fourth level. The place was deserted this time of the evening when everyone had gone home or out on the town. Not even the tick of a cooling engine invaded the quiet emptiness.

Maddie halted within sight of her corner stall, offering swift and unimpeded getaway. The ginger-brown front section of a 1972 Oldsmobile Cutlass coupe poked out from behind its neighboring late-model Sebring. She slipped the pack onto one shoulder and fished her keys from an outside zipper pocket, then pointed the remote control toward the vehicle and pressed a button. The Cutlass purred to life as gentle and unassuming as its appearance. No fireworks.

She exhaled a long breath. They hadn't found this vehicle. It wasn't registered to Madison Jameson or Madeleine Jerrard, but she'd learned to be safe rather than sorry with her hunters. Their noses were sharp and their reach was long. She hurried toward the vehicle. The sooner this city faded in her rearview mirror, the better.

The engine revved and the Cutlass sprang forward. Maddie skidded to a halt feet from the grill, bitterness coating her tongue. Someone sat behind the wheel. No way to discern more than a silhouette in the dimness, but whoever it was couldn't be a friend. She had no more of those.

Maddie whirled and ran. The vehicle followed, and a voice called her full name—her real name. Sure, they'd mock her identity at the end. No bullet for her. Just a hit and run with her own car. A greasy spot on the pavement.

She wasn't about to let them win that easily. As she ran, her hand dove inside her pack and closed around the handle of a 10 mm Glock pistol. She tossed the pack and disengaged the safety on the pistol.

"Maddie!" the male voice called again. Too familiar. And impossible!

Her racing feet jerked to a halt, and she pivoted on her heel, Glock extended in both hands. The Oldsmobile's tires locked, and the car skidded toward her. The scent of burnt rubber met Maddie's nostrils as she leaped up and forward. The vehicle rocked to a halt, bumper covering the spot where she'd been standing. She landed atop the hood on her knees and the knuckles of one fist. The other arm trained the Glock on the driver.

He lifted his hands, palms out, lips pressed into a tight line.

Blood pounded in Maddie's ears and blackness edged her vision. It *was* him.

The most gorgeous man on the planet. He was supposed to be dead, but he was alive. She should shoot him.

TWO

Chris Mason stared past the gun barrel and into the tawny eyes of Madeleine Jerrard. His insides melted. She could put a bullet in him right now, and he'd die a happy man. What kind of a fool did that make him?

God, this has got to be Your best joke on me yet.

He knew better than to fall for the subject of an investigation. Years back, as an eager-eyed neophyte in the reporting business, he'd paid too high a price for that mistake and vowed never again. He gritted his teeth as if a tense jaw could steel him against the unwanted stirrings in his heart for this woman who could kill him in a heartbeat—and had good reason to do it. Or thought she did. A year of stretching every investigative skill and resource, and he'd found her. But at what cost? They were both on enemy radar now.

"What are you doing in my car?"

Her demand reached him through the driver's-side window he'd opened in order to call her name.

He shrugged. "Trying not to run you over, but this thing's got more power in the tap of a toe than my toasted rental had if I floored it."

Maddie grinned and slid off the hood of the Oldsmobile. She stood a few feet from the open window, gun lowered, but not all the way. "Ginger looks like granny wheels but drives like a Ferrari." The gun lifted. "How did you find this car?"

"It wasn't easy, and it looked hopeless, but then I found something in my notes from those weeks I spent with the team during preparation for the mission."

"What was that?" Interest sparked in Maddie's gaze though her tone wielded a sharp edge.

"If you recall, I asked everyone a trivia question for a human-interest angle I was hoping to develop. You said the two people you admired most in history were Harriet Tubman, because she risked her life to free others, and Joan of Arc, because she took up the sword for what she believed was a divine cause. When that piece of information clicked in my brain, and I ran a DMV search, guess what I found in San Antonio?"

"A vehicle registered to Joan Tubman."

"Bingo! A little more digging uncovered a long-term parking space rental for the same vehicle. But don't worry. I handled the searches personally. Our mutual *friends* don't know about this car."

"So you admit they're your friends."

Chris snorted. "Don't you recognize sarcasm when you hear it? Friends don't blow up friends."

Maddie frowned, and her gaze scanned his face. "Unless there's a deeper game."

"What might that be?"

"I'll let you know when I figure it out. Answer me this—how did you get inside? I always lock my vehicles."

Chris smirked. "Hanging out with your unit taught me skills for functioning in enemy territory, like reaching the locking mechanism of an older model car with a wedge and a coat hanger. All I needed to do was let you start the car. I never did get a lesson on hot-wiring."

She sniffed and her eyes narrowed. "Why weren't you French fried in that sedan at the hotel? I thought you were dead."

"No such luck, sweetheart."

She scowled.

"You saved my life," he continued.

"Me!"

"Ever since Mexico, I use the remote start before I get behind the wheel. A tip you shared."

"Hurray for me. Now, get out." She motioned with the gun.

Chris shook his head. "You'll have to pull that trigger and dump my dead body. You're stuck with me. Apparently, my search for you picked up a tail, and they're trying to kill me, too."

"Thanks for leading them to my hidey-hole." Her lips thinned. "How do I know you're not still working for them?"

"Still?" Irritation spiked in Chris's breast. "Did you forget that I was investigated and exonerated?"

"Not by me."

"Obviously." Chris scowled. "Maddie, they tried to *kill* me! Doesn't that prove my innocence?"

"I know I'm not the one who betrayed the coalition. Everyone else is dead, except the investigative reporter the big shots saddled us with during the touchiest mission of our lives. Do the math." She raised her chin. "Attempting to blow you to kingdom come proves you've made them nervous that you may be a liability—nothing more."

Chris's molars ground together. "Since I've clearly made their hit list, we might as well go on the lam together until we can figure out a way to put a stop to this evil."

"Stop it? That's what we were doing in Nuevo Laredo until someone tipped off the cartel to our location."

"That someone was not me." Chris glared at Maddie. "Believe it or not, I may be the only person who can and will help you expose the cartel's state-side allies. Our survival depends on delivering them, gift-wrapped, to the Senate subcommittee."

Maddie sniffed. "The same committee that publicly blamed my unit in order to save their pitiful reputations over the failed mission *they* authorized? In case you haven't noticed, my career in the army is blown to the winds like dandelion fluff. And apparently someone thinks I might remember something from the night of the attack that is worth hunting me down."

Chris leveled a long look at Maddie. Her high cheekbones stood out above tensed muscles, and her nostrils flared beneath a molten amber gaze. She looked wild and beautiful…and off-limits to this hard-nosed reporter. *And don't you forget it,* he told his heart. This was about a story, maybe the biggest of his career, but one wrong move and he'd see nothing of Maddie but dust. *Patience, Mason, patience.*

"Whatever you think of me," he said, "both our lives are in danger from the same people. I won't last ten minutes without you."

"You said a mouthful, buckaroo."

"And you will never be able to lead a normal life until we gather enough solid evidence about what really happened at the Rio Grande for me to go public with it. If anyone knows how to go about getting that evidence, I do, but I need your help to stay alive that long."

Maddie's generous lower lip disappeared between her teeth and her gaze darted away, then returned. The chill in her eyes skewered his hopes. He'd taken his best shot and lost.

"Shove over." She motioned with the gun, then trotted toward the spot where she'd tossed her pack.

Chris complied in haste, twisting his long body into crazy contortions to surmount the center console and settle into the bucket seat on the passenger side. He wasn't about to step out of the vehicle and have her change her mind, then leave him sucking exhaust. Her reasons for letting him ride along, given what she thought of him, were likely as layered as her personality, but he wouldn't find them out until she chose to share them.

Maddie climbed in, maneuvered the stick shift, and they drove, smooth as glass, out of the parking garage. "Where to, Mr. Investigative Reporter?"

"Grab I-35 south toward Laredo."

Maddie frowned, but headed the vehicle in the proper direction to catch the Interstate. "Back to the scene of the crime?"

"It's a good place to start."

"And the last place our enemies would think to look for us." She grinned wolfishly. "I may not trust you, but I like the way you think."

"You used to like a lot more about me than that."

Chris could have slapped himself. Why did he shoot off his mouth about the mutual attraction they'd danced around since the day they were first introduced? So what if they'd flirted with their eyes and sometimes their banter during the training days before the mission? Romance between them was strictly off-limits.

"Don't remind me of my bad judgment." She shot him a glare that could have sizzled bacon.

"Is there some reason you don't think someone on the Mexican side of the equation could have betrayed our location?"

She snorted. "They're as dead as the rest of the U.S.

forces. Only a member of the coalition team on the ground with us would have known which of half a dozen designated safe zones we chose to bivouac that final night before the assault on the cartel was to begin. We operated under close cover for a reason. Even the Mexicans know plenty of their officials are on the cartel's payroll. What our good U.S. citizens don't like to face is that drug money talks as loudly on our side of the border. Government pension isn't *that* good."

"I hear you." Chris nodded. "That's why I want to start by talking to the DEA agents in the Laredo field office. I ferreted out their home addresses before I took my flight to San Antonio."

"Good thought." She ghosted a grim smile. "They lost comrades. Some of them were in on the planning phase. Some may even be dirty. If anyone can dig out a nugget that the FBI investigation missed, it's The Man with the Golden Tongue from *World News*."

She laughed but Chris frowned. He slumped against his seat, closed his eyes and pretended to fall asleep. The real thing eluded him, as usual. For the past year, exhaustion and a latent sense of desperation had dogged his every step. Maddie had no idea how many sleepless nights he'd spent since that horror in the desert.

When he slept the dreams came. The scream of incoming mortar rounds. Visions of smoke and fire and the scent of burning flesh. Worse, he saw her broken and bloodied body sprawled on the ground in the middle of the encampment. He'd carried her in his arms away from the war zone to save her life, but in the end she'd saved *his*. Someone had followed them away from the camp and started taking potshots at them. Maddie revived long enough to draw her sidearm and return fire. Did she remember any of that?

Clearly not. And he couldn't explain right now. Anything he said or did was suspect.

In her mind, the fact that he was the only one to escape that night without harm equated complicity with the attack. The logic made sense on the surface…only that wasn't what happened, and he had no idea how to convince her otherwise.

Lord, you've got to help me here. I have no idea how to regain this woman's trust.

Maddie glanced at her passenger. He was pretending to sleep. The twitch of a muscle under his jaw betrayed him. He was frustrated, probably angry with her for not buying into his innocence the minute he gazed at her with those baby blues and exercised his honeyed voice. She'd been tempted. Mightily. But too many of her friends had lost their lives for her to trust anyone involved who was still breathing. Not until she knew for sure what really happened.

Chris said he wanted to help with that. Well, all right. He had the skills. She didn't. She'd give him some rope and see where it led. Letting him into her car, inviting him back into her life, had to number among the gutsiest things she'd ever done, because now she couldn't trust herself any more than she trusted him. The attraction was too strong. She'd have to make sure her head stayed in charge.

Right! Like hugging a viper ever turned out well.

Her foot itched to press on the brakes. She should pull over and toss him out. One fact stopped her. Death dogged her trail, with or without him by her side. What was that old saying? *Keep your friends close and your enemies closer.* The *frenemy* in her passenger seat would betray himself one way or another soon enough.

"Did you soup up this car yourself?"

His question jolted Maddie. He suddenly wanted conversation? She glanced toward the passenger seat and found him sitting up straight and alert, subterfuge laid aside for the moment. If that was the way he wanted to play it, she could be cool and cordial, too.

Maddie shook her head. "Ginger was my big brother's pride and joy. He restored her chassis to near original, but supercharged her insides. Then he was deployed to Afghanistan, and a roadside bomb ended his life before he got to enjoy the fruits of his labor. I inherited her, and she's one possession I'm not about to give up, even when I'm on the run for my life."

"I don't blame you. Pretty smart, though, selling Ginger to yourself under an assumed name and changing the license plate numbers."

"You figured that out from your Department of Motor Vehicles search?" A shiver slithered down her back. Could someone else follow the same trail? Sure, if they dug too deeply into the background of the buyer of record, Joan Tubman, and discovered her to be a phantom. Keeping Ginger might rank among the top stupid choices of her life. So be it. Her hands clenched the steering wheel.

Chris patted the dashboard like a man caresses a beloved pet. "As long as you have Ginger, you have a tangible connection to your brother."

Maddie awarded him a wide-eyed stare. "Do you have a degree in psychology, too?"

"Comes with the reporter territory." He smiled with one side of his mouth. "You get to know a thing or two about how the human soul ticks. Your attachment to the vehicle is natural. I respect that."

The backs of Maddie's eyes stung, and she glued her gaze to the road. "I suppose your research told you Jason was the last living member of my immediate family. The news of his death reached me while I was in the hospital, recovering from the Rio Grande. My parents and only sibling are gone, my nearest relatives are a few scattered cousins and an aunt who lives on the other side of the country, and the army has divorced me. I'm a free agent. Works well for someone on the run."

She finished in a glib tone but made the mistake of glancing at him. The compassion in his eyes nearly gave birth to the tears that lurked behind hers. Every once in a while, like now, it was daunting to think there was no one in the world who would miss her if she was gone, but she couldn't reveal her vulnerability to this man. He'd take full advantage of it to get his story.

Her gaze narrowed. So that was the motive behind his dogged search for her. An Emmy wasn't enough? She was his one-way ticket to another sensational story. He probably hadn't figured on joining her in her enemies' crosshairs.

"You're slick as a weasel in the weeds. Do you know that?" She sent him a sidelong look. "You thought I'd buy into the idea that you've stepped back into this mess for truth, justice, and the American way. But it's all about the story, isn't it? Expose the mastermind behind the Rio Grande Massacre, and win another award. A scoop like this ought to be worth at least a Peabody."

Tenderness evaporated from his face. Maddie's heart jolted, and she tasted the loss. What was the matter with her? She didn't want warmth from him, did she? His kindness was dangerous to her peace of mind. When he looked at her like he'd welcome her into his arms, she yearned too badly to go there. Then why did it bother her that she'd hurt him?

His skin darkened. "I thought you considered me in the employ of the mastermind. Why would I dare expose the person or persons who could expose *me* as a traitor to my country?"

"Good question." She lifted her chin. "Like you, I'm hoping for answers on this joy ride."

"Like you said earlier, I know *I* didn't betray the coalition team. But unlike you, I don't assume the other survivor did."

"Survivor? If you mean I'm alive, yes, but I did a tough stint in the hospital. You? Your hair didn't even get ruffled in the cartel's attack. How did that happen?"

An odd look passed across Chris's face, half earnest, half eager, with a hint of baffled frustration thrown in. He opened his mouth, and Maddie waited for a revelation regarding his survival. Like where he was hiding while her team was being slaughtered.

But he turned his face away and stared out his passenger-side window. "I don't know how the cartel got word of our location, but I intend to find out."

Maddie suppressed her irritation. Evidently the information highway didn't work two directions with a reporter.

She forced a grin and kept her eyes on the road. "At last, we agree on something, Mr. Mason."

Rousing a DEA agent at midnight in the privacy of his home would send a tide of reaction up the chain of command. Possibly provoke a rash move by someone who would prefer to remain hidden.

At least, that was the theory, and Chris intended to test it. He gripped the door handle as Maddie pulled the Cutlass to the curb outside Agent Clyde Ramsey's two-story house in a modest subdivision of Laredo, Texas. She killed the headlights but left the engine running and fixed a steady stare on Chris.

"Wait here," he said.

"Not going to happen. I want to catch every word either of you speaks."

"It might be a good idea if our enemies don't yet realize we've joined forces."

"Maybe." She frowned. "Here's the deal. I'll lurk in the shadows while you knock on his door. Do your best to hold your chat right there. But if you move inside, I'm stepping out and coming in, too."

Chris frowned. Not the best plan, but he wasn't likely to get a better concession from someone who didn't trust him. "Deal." He held out his hand.

She brushed his palm with her fingertips. An intake of breath hissed between her lips, while a minor earthquake went through him. Did she feel the tremor, too? Or did the tentative touch—uncharacteristic of her usual forthrightness—mean that she found him loathsome? Impossible to tell with Maddie, and he had no time to ponder the answers. She was getting out of the car, her Glock in one hand and a flashlight in the other.

Chris hastily exited the Cutlass onto the sidewalk that led up to the house. Quiet draped the area, except for a soft shush of traffic noise from the Interstate only a mile distant. The scent of verbena drifted on the breeze, the only thing innocent and winsome about this moment.

He remembered Ramsey from the planning phase of the operation. The guy liked to talk tough and throw his weight around, but original thought was pretty negligible. If he was a participant in the tragedy on the Rio Grande, he was an order taker, not a mastermind. Chris's research told him Ramsey was a family man with a wife and two half-grown kids. Not surprising that his house lay dark... or maybe not completely. As Chris moved up the sidewalk he discerned a faint bluish glow filtering around the edges of heavy blinds on a front right-side window. Was someone up watching television? Insomnia or a guilty conscience? Chris's steps quickened.

They reached the front stoop, and true to her word, Maddie faded into the shadows against the house. Chris rapped on the door. No response. He hammered, waited and then his finger headed toward the doorbell, but a light flipped on in the foyer before his pointer hit the button. He stood quietly, staring at the peephole, while whoever was on the other side scoped him out.

A lock rattled, the door eased open several inches, and a pair of smoke-colored eyes set deep in a bulldog face peered out. Their gazes locked. The DEA agent wore a pair of lightweight pajamas, and the hand that wasn't holding the door was hidden behind his back. Chris's scalp prickled. Was he armed? Maddie's close presence might be more necessary than he'd thought.

"Surprised to see me?" he said.

"You're that reporter who's supposed to be dead. Why aren't you?"

"I wasn't in the car when it blew."

"Yeah, I knew that much. The late news said they found no body in the vehicle. The cops have you listed as a missing person. What do you want here?"

"What does any reporter want? Answers. Only now, getting them is personal."

"That leads you to me how?" The smoky eyes narrowed.

"The attempt on my life was related to the Rio Grande Massacre. I've been searching for Madeleine Jerrard, and I was getting close. Someone didn't care to have me find her."

"There you have your answer." Ramsey let out a piglike grunt. "It was Jerrard. She wasn't right in the head after the Rio, and she tried to take you out. Those rangers are more dangerous than a nest of rattlers. Better back off, newsman."

"Not until I uncover the truth about how the cartel found the encampment."

"Don't you listen to your own network's news? They reported months ago that the investigators concluded the ranger scout got careless and led the cartel forces back to the camp."

"I don't buy that story. Never have. I spent weeks observing and cataloguing the preparation phase. I'm not easy to impress, but that ranger team did it for me. As soon as the need for secrecy was past, I expected to share the story of their triumph with the world." Chris leaned closer to the DEA agent. A faint scent of whiskey teased his nostrils. What kept this guy up nursing booze in the night? "I didn't like being left with a story of posthumous heroism. My cameraman was killed in the first barrage, and I want to know who's really responsible."

Ramsey stiffened and drew back. "What? You think I had something to do with it?" A blue vein pulsed in the man's forehead. "Don't forget, my office lost several good agents."

"Are you saying that no one in the Laredo DEA office could possibly be dirty?"

"I'm not saying they *couldn't*. I'm saying they *aren't*. Including me. Now get off my property, or I'm calling the cops. Right after I fill your pants with buckshot." He pulled a shotgun from behind his back and cradled it in the crook of his elbow.

Chris lifted both hands and backed away a step. "I'll go, but I'm not through digging."

Ramsey's gaze took on a mean glint. "You will be if you enjoy breathing."

"Is that a threat?"

"Naw. A prediction."

"Fine. Now here's my prediction. Whatever's eating you up inside is going to take you down with a stroke or an ulcer, or else it's going to trash your career with a DUI."

Ramsey growled and started to raise the shotgun. Chris turned on his heel and hustled down the sidewalk, shoulder blades tingling. He didn't look back. His life was in Maddie's hands if the DEA agent decided to try pulling the trigger. He reached the car, which was still running, climbed in the driver's side and drove off. She was smart enough to slip away and meet him around the corner. He pulled over to the curb and waited. Sure enough, she slid into the passenger seat less than a minute later.

"Good job of rattling the bones in the closet." She gave that throaty chuckle that turned him to molten putty, only he'd never let her know it. "Now we'll see what falls out." Her hand on his stopped him from putting the car into gear. "I had no idea you didn't buy the official story about our team scout, Don Avery. That guy could sneak up on a mouse, tie a ribbon to its tail and slip away without the critter ever knowing he was close. There's no way he led the cartel to our bivouac."

She took her hand away, but the warmth of her touch lingered. He smiled as he headed the Cutlass out of the neighborhood.

"I'm impressed that you didn't get in his face when he was spouting that stuff about your unit."

"We do learn a little self-discipline in the army." Her tone was dry. "It sticks, even when we're not right in the head anymore."

"Forget that stupid remark." Chris chopped the air with his hand. "I think you've made a remarkable recovery."

"Thanks." The word dripped gratitude.

A lump formed beneath Chris's breastbone. It had probably been a long time since someone who cared had offered her a vote of confidence. He'd give anything to chase away the shadows in those beautiful, tawny eyes. Maybe uncovering the real traitor would accomplish that, because he couldn't offer her the comfort of a personal relationship. Last time he'd blurred the lines between his personal and professional lives the wrong person took a bullet.

"Could you stand a snack break?" His question came out a little husky.

"Sure." The answer echoed his tight-throated tone.

They stopped at an all-night convenience store to use the facilities, put on gas and grab a bite to eat. Then they headed toward their next destination—the home of Edgar Jackson, the other DEA agent who participated in the planning but not the performance of the ill-fated Rio Grande operation.

"He's divorced. Lives alone," Chris informed Maddie as they parked in front of a dinky rambler wedged between a colonial and a Southwestern-style stucco home.

He walked up to the front door while Maddie disappeared into the darkness.

Standing on the stoop, Chris's insides clenched. "Maddie?"

"Yo," she answered out of the shadows.

"Something's not right here. The front door is ajar."

"Don't touch anything." She appeared beside him. "Step to the side of the door like you've seen in all the cop shows and call the guy's name."

He did as he was told while she stood with her back pressed to the wall on the other side of the door. Silence answered Chris's call. The heavy stillness stole his breath. What was that faint metallic smell?

Maddie sniffed. "Blood," she murmured, answering his question. "Stay back." She moved in front of the door, gun at ready angle, then shoved the door wide with her shoulder and clicked on her flashlight.

A man's body sprawled, faceup, in the foyer. Beside one wide-flung arm lay a paperback novel with a thin scrap of colorful cardstock paper on the floor nearby. The other hand clutched what looked like a matching scrap in its fist. Gunpowder speckled the man's slack face around a black hole in his forehead. The blood they'd smelled spread in a crimson pool beneath the body's head.

Bile burned the back of Chris's throat. Agent Edgar Jackson wouldn't be answering any questions.

THREE

Death. Maddie'd had her fill of it, but here it lay again, staring with sightless eyes. She suppressed an internal shiver.

A distant sound brought her head up. Sirens.

She grabbed Chris's arm. He stood mesmerized by the body. She shook him.

"We've got to go. Someone has called the cops. Maybe a neighbor heard the shot. That blood's fresh. The killing couldn't have happened more than a few minutes ago."

Chris turned a fierce blue gaze on her. "He was silenced because we were coming for answers."

"Maybe. Or else he stepped on some dealer's toes because of his job. We don't have time for debate right now. And I sure don't want to discuss the issue with the police if they arrive to find us standing over a dead DEA agent."

"What's that in his hand?" He pointed at the scrap Edgar Jackson clutched in his fist.

"What difference does it make?" Chris's reporter curiosity was going to land them in a cell at the local jail, sitting ducks for their enemies.

He broke free of her grip on his arm and bent over the body.

"Come on!" Those sirens were getting scary close.

"All right. All right." He waved at her but didn't move or look up.

She clicked off the flashlight. "Enough sleuthing, Sherlock. We're out of time."

He let out a disgusted snort, rose, and charged out the door ahead of her.

"Finally!" she muttered and followed him toward the car. "I'm driving."

He piled into the passenger seat. She slid on her rear across Ginger's hood, then took her place at the wheel. Lights off, she skimmed the Cutlass away from the curb. Within seconds the units would be in view of the house. She took the first available turn. *No!* A cul-de-sac. *Wait! What was that?* A dirt drive angled off through a vacant lot between a pair of the houses. Maddie turned onto it.

The drive petered out behind the neighborhood at the edge of an open field. Maddie applied the brakes and studied the situation. The full moon revealed a couple of large pieces of machinery hunkered to their left, and directly ahead, a swath of excavation possibly several feet deep and a few car-lengths wide. A new subdivision was about to be born. Multiple sirens chorused not more than a stone's throw distant.

She looked toward her passenger and sensed more than saw his return gaze.

"I'm game for the next move. Your call," he said.

Maddie's heart expanded. Chris was bold as any ranger, smart enough to know he wasn't one, and too comfortable in his manhood to be threatened by ranger skills in a female package. A rare combination, as she'd had cause to learn from a few dating fiascos. Not that she had the least interest in romance with a reporter who was playing her for the sake of a story, especially when he might have had a pivotal hand in the deaths of her brothers-in-arms.

Maybe he was tricked into betraying their location.

She batted away the feeble excuse. Either Chris Mason was a full-on traitor or he had phenomenal luck, surviving both the attack at the Rio Grande and the attempt on his life at the hotel.

"Have you ever watched any reruns of that old show *Dukes of Hazzard?*" she asked.

"One of my dad's favorites."

"The General Lee's got nothing on Ginger."

"Which am I? Bo or Luke Duke?"

"Take your pick. I'm Daisy. Tighten your seat belt."

She threw Ginger in Reverse, took her back a few yards and then opened her up. The engine's purr rose to a growl. The landscape rushed toward them to be gobbled beneath the Oldsmobile's tires. The rough terrain chattered her teeth together. Then they went airborne, and the bottom fell out of Maddie's stomach.

"Yeee-haaa!" Her passenger's rebel yell brought a grin to her face. He looked more like Luke, but evidently he'd decided to be Bo.

The wheels met terra firma, and Maddie's head grazed the roof. Pressure steady on the accelerator, they zipped across the remainder of the field, bumped over a curb and hit pavement. Maddie cramped the wheel to the right and fishtailed them onto a residential street.

"We made it!" Chris's grin came through in his voice. "If there's anything fun about this situation, that was it."

"That was nothing. You should try flying over a hill on a dirt bike."

"Anytime."

"It's a date."

The breath stalled in Maddie's throat. Why had such intimate terminology escaped her mouth? Maybe because this was the way they had bantered in the days of excitement leading up to what should have been a resounding victory in the war on drugs. Before her world got blown up and everyone became a suspect. She stole a glance toward the shadowed figure of her passenger. His gaze faced straight ahead, and he had the good sense not to respond to her quip.

The first time she'd seen Chris her team had been debarking from their air transport at the secret training facility in the Arizona desert. Their orders were simple and straightforward, just the way the army liked it. Her team was to meet with a handpicked task force of DEA agents and Mexican federales, forge a plan, then go after the Ortiz Cartel, capture whoever would surrender, and those who wouldn't—well, they had the sanction of two governments to wipe them out like the nest of vipers they were. But then this reporter was thrust into their midst.

The day preparation began, Maddie had leaped from the chopper, full pack on her back, and trotted behind her commanding officer toward the underground bunkers that would house them for the duration of their planning and training. Chris had been standing in his shirtsleeves next to his stocky cameraman, watching her unit pass, coffee-colored hair whipping every which way in the airstream from the whirling helicopter blades. His deep blue stare had collided with hers, sending sparks to her toenails.

The team CO had nearly blown a gasket when he discovered the bureaucrats upstairs had saddled them with a civilian reporter to document their activities from start to finish. But Chris had refused to back down in front of a man whose bark sent chills down the backs of hardened G.I.s, and he'd won a smidgeon of grudging respect. Then he threw himself into whatever was on the docket, even attempting some of the grueling training activities. Sometimes he didn't do half bad, other times he made a complete fool of himself with good grace, earning more respect.

By the time their final orders came through, Chris was accepted by the hodgepodge strike team of rangers, Mexican law enforcement personnel and DEA agents as nearly one of their own. Then they were moved to a top-secret bivouac on the Mexico side of the Rio Grande, poised to strike the very next day...except the cartel had been tipped off to their location and descended with high-tech weaponry that used to be available only to the military of legitimate governments.

The cartel considered itself an authority of its own, superseding the civil governments. They made their own rules and broke them at will, and either coerced or bought cooperation from everyone necessary to conduct their slimy international trade. Had Chris been bought before or after he wormed his way into the good graces of her team?

What if he's innocent? The question echoed in her mind and sucked her breath away.

The longer they were thrown together, the more her conviction about his betrayal weakened and the stronger her attraction toward this way too charming man grew. *Coward!* She flinched at her mental blast toward herself. The brave men and women who died at the Rio Grande deserved better than her vacillation. But didn't she deserve a chance at happiness with someone she could love and trust?

Futility gripped her by the throat. What she wanted and what she could have always seemed like opposite things.

The pink rays of dawn roused Chris from a fitful slumber. He blinked his eyes open. They were parked in a far corner of a Walmart lot, trying to grab a few *z*'s.

He looked toward Maddie, snoozing in the driver's seat.

Her head leaned against her side window. The sun's beams outlined her profile, so delicate and fine for such a tough woman. Maddie didn't think of herself as beautiful, but she was. Not in the classic sense, but Barbie-doll looks didn't interest him. He liked the strong, clean lines of her nose and jaw and the graceful length of her neck beneath the seashell curve of her ear. And that mouth. His dreams weren't always about blood and death. Sometimes—for just an instant—he tasted those full, firm lips.

What would it be like to taste them for real?

Forget it, buddy! But the heart was a rebellious organ and resisted his stern command.

Maddie stirred and lifted her head. She met his gaze. He smiled, but she grimaced and rolled her jaw.

"My mouth is so dry it thinks we must be back in the Iraqi desert."

"Texas in the summertime isn't much better. Good thing it cools off at night, or we'd be roasting right now."

She gave him a stare that questioned his sanity. "Have you ever been in Iraq?"

"I haven't had the privilege. I'm not a foreign correspondent."

"One hundred twenty in the shade makes a Texas summer feel like a day at the spa."

Chris chuckled. "Guess I'll have to cancel my vacation plans to Baghdad."

She shook her head with a muted smile. A low rumble carried to Chris's ears, and her face turned pink.

Maddie pressed a hand to her abdomen. "I'm hungry, as well as dry."

"Ditto."

They went into the Walmart to freshen up in the bathrooms. Chris caught up with Maddie browsing in the produce section.

"What do you want for breakfast?" She hefted a peach. "These look awesome to me."

Chris took the fruit from her and set it in the bin. "I may not be a soldier but I need some he-man sustenance in a sit-down restaurant."

Her brow puckered. "What about keeping a low profile? Someone could recognize you, and then our enemies would have a read on our location."

Chris shrugged. "After last night's visit to Agent Ramsey, they already know I'm in town—or soon will. The guy will hardly keep our presence a secret, and the news will filter through the system pretty quickly. Besides, anyone could recognize my televised mug anytime, anywhere…even standing in a store like this."

Maddie's gaze swept the area, and she heaved a breath. "Roger that, but we'll have to stay on the move so we can't be pinned down."

"Uh…Roger that." He grinned. "Now how about a rib-sticking breakfast?"

They adjourned to a restaurant down the road.

"What next, Sherlock?" she asked as the waitress withdrew from delivering cups of stout black coffee.

Chris pulled the colorful scrap of card stock from his jeans pocket.

Her narrowed gaze focused on what he held in his hand. "You didn't!" The words spat out through gritted teeth.

Chris's neck warmed. "I'm a reporter. Digging is what I do." At least if he talked to her about this in a public place she couldn't murder him, could she?

"At a crime scene?" Her voice rose to a muted screech.

He leaned toward her across the table. "Advertise to the world, will you?"

She crossed her arms on a huff, a mulish set to her jaw. Fortunately, they were seated a good distance from any other patrons. The restaurant wasn't busy this early in the morning.

"It was an instinctive move," he said. "I snatched the stray piece from the floor, not the other half in the dead guy's hand. We needed to leave, but if this scrap of paper can lead us closer to the truth, isn't it worth the risk?"

"Taking anything from a crime scene could put us behind bars." Her words emerged low but sharp. "Not that we'd ever have the opportunity for a trial. As stationary targets, we won't survive that long."

"What if taking this could keep us from getting dead? I don't want either of us to add to the body count."

"You really think Jackson was killed to keep him from talking?"

"Don't you?"

She canted her head and seconds passed. "Maybe," she conceded.

"It's too big of a coincidence for this journalist to swallow that within an hour after we confront one of the DEA planners of our intended assault on the cartel, the other planner is dead and left for us to find."

"Do you think someone meant for us to take the rap for the killing?"

"Me, anyway. Hopefully, they don't yet realize we're a team."

Her expression shuttered as her gaze focused on her coffee cup. Did she object to his use of the word *team?* The term implied trust and interdependence.

Finally, she lifted her gaze to his. "Whoever planned the betrayal of our coalition forces is very smart. Since we're both known to be alive, and we've disappeared at the same time, it's a fair guess this person suspects we're together."

"Suspecting and knowing are two different things."

"We need to listen to the news and find out what they're saying about the murder."

"That and visit the nearest library."

"A library?"

"The novel on the floor beside Agent Jackson was a Western, but he was marking his place with this bookmark promoting a memoir about the Vietnam War. A lot of soldiers came out of that war either addicted to drugs and/or savvy about drug distribution. Maybe the author has some connection to what happened on the Rio."

Maddie frowned. "I doubt the connection could be that simple or direct. I mean, Jackson would have had all of a few seconds after he opened his front door to realize he was going to die. By what coincidence would he be holding a bookmark promoting a book written by his killer?"

"I can't answer that question...yet."

Maddie shrugged. "A slim lead is better than no lead."

Get a lid on your enthusiasm, would you? Chris contented himself with thinking his frustration rather than speaking it aloud. Just as well. The waitress was approaching with their breakfasts. A gurgle from his stomach welcomed the savory smells of bacon, hash browns, fried eggs and pancakes. He winced toward Maddie's choice of whole-grain toast, a fruit cup and a veggie omelet.

"You've been busy in the past year," she said as she snagged a piece of omelet with her fork.

He raised his eyebrows toward her, and a flush worked its way from beneath her collar onto her cheeks.

She lifted her chin. "I mean you've gone after more stories than this one since last we met. You didn't spend *all* your time looking for *me*."

Chris savored a bite of hash browns then leaned back in his chair. "My hunt for you was private—on my own time. The station had plenty of what they considered *new* news for me to investigate and report."

"Like the David Greene case?"

Ah, so that's where this conversation was going. The lurid business of a Texas oil millionaire under suspicion of strangling his girlfriend had dominated the airwaves for quite some time. Too long, in his opinion.

"You followed that one, did you?" He drizzled syrup onto his pancakes, keeping half an eye cocked toward his companion.

Her stare skewered him. "I thought it was very interesting that your segments were the only ones that left room to believe the louse might be innocent."

"You have something against unbiased media coverage?"

"I have something against killers getting away with murder just because they're rich and can hire slick lawyers."

"Is that what you think happened?"

"It's what everybody thinks happened…except you! What fries my goose is that Greene didn't end up charged with anything, even though he was found in the same room with the dead body."

"Passed out cold, I might remind you." Chris wagged his fork at her.

Maddie sniffed. "So the booze and pills knocked him out *after* he went nuts on his girlfriend."

He laid down his fork and crossed his arms over his chest. "David Greene was tried and convicted in the court of public opinion, but it might do the public good to realize that there could be a reason why he was never formally charged."

"Insufficient evidence. Blah. Blah." She wrinkled her nose and took a swig of her orange juice. "I suppose it's just as well that they wait to haul the slime into court until they have a case that will convict…if that ever happens."

"I'll be happy if enough evidence is uncovered to convict the *right* person—whoever that may be. Even David himself is unsure what happened that night."

"David? First-name basis, huh? I noticed you were the only reporter Greene would allow to interview him. Huge coup for your network. You're all about grabbing those."

Chris frowned. She was back to needling him with her suspicions about his career-building motives for tracking her down.

She leaned toward him. "Do you have some sort of inside track with this creep?"

"If you must know," he said on a sigh, "Davie Greene was a hooligan who lived in the same town as me when I was a snot-nosed kid. Way before his Apache grandfather died and left him a swatch of sand and cactus that turned out to be floating on a lake of oil. We went to the same elementary school. David was a wild child, but one thing I remember about him, he couldn't tolerate anyone picking on girls or weaker kids. He ended up with more bloody noses than I can count from standing up to bullies who were tormenting other children. We weren't close friends or anything, but I rather admired his rowdy gallantry."

A sharp chuckle left her lips. "So this candidate for knighthood grew up, got rich quick and power corrupted his saintly character."

"Saintly? Hardly. Just an underdog who defended underdogs."

"And who you happened to know from back in the day. Lucky break for you and *World News*."

Chris bit back angry but useless words. There was a lot more to the story, but nothing that stood much chance of changing her opinion of him or David. How could he explain that he owed it to his network, as well as the natural-born newsman inside him, to pursue stories how and where they were presented? But that didn't negate his personal quest for answers about the Rio Grande Massacre, regardless of whether or not he was ever credited with another word of the coverage. Fat chance she'd put any stock in his higher motives when she saw him as someone who would take advantage of a personal connection with a killer in order to bolster his career and boost his network's ratings.

Uneasy silence fell between them, and they both attacked their food like it was a mutual enemy. As they finished their breakfasts, Maddie's head lifted, and her gaze fixed on something beyond his shoulder.

"Don't turn to look," she said softly, "but we've got company on your six."

"My six?" Oh, yes, that meant behind him in military-speak. Chris swiveled his head and caught his breath. A pair of uniformed police officers were striding through the front door of the restaurant. He quickly turned back toward Maddie. "Cops!"

Her gaze held stern reproach. "I told you not to look."

"I'm a reporter. I'm trained to look anywhere someone tells me not to look."

She rolled her eyes.

"Where are they now?"

"Heading for us like we're a pair of homing beacons." Her face went grim. "You'd better hope they don't arrest us on the spot. Forget a charge of tampering with a crime scene. What you've got in your pocket will convict us of murder in any court of law."

FOUR

Maddie stared at the morsels remaining on her plate as doom trod closer…closer. Her muscles tensed and tingled into combat mode. Clearly, her body wasn't getting the memo from her common sense. There was no way she could resist arrest.

Even if submitting to lockup meant certain death?

The policemen reached their table and strode past with scarcely a glance in their direction. Maddie's head went light as a helium balloon. Then she remembered to breathe.

Chris sent her a wicked grin. "Don't look now, but the officers have taken a table on your six. Guess they're here for breakfast like the rest of us law-abiding citizens."

Maddie scowled. "Let's get out of here while the getting is good."

She began to swivel out of her chair, but a shadow loomed over them and froze her in her seat. One of the officers. Her throat closed against an involuntary squeak.

The stocky man gazed down at them—well, at Chris anyway—thick brows drawn together. "Excuse me, but would you be Christopher Mason from *World News?*"

Chris leaned back in his chair and answered the man's stare with a steady, cool expression. "That would be me. What can I do for you, officer?"

Maddie's teeth ground together. If Chris possessed this level of acting ability, she was right to suspect he could be hiding his complicity in the Rio Grande Massacre and playing her for a story at the same time. Then why did that conclusion feel so wrong in her gut? She shook herself inwardly. Better to keep listening to her head—safer for everyone if she trusted no one.

The policeman scratched under his ear and offered a small grimace. "Are you aware that the vehicle you rented at the airport blew up yesterday?"

Chris nodded. "Fortunately, I wasn't in it at the time."

"Yes, but sir, you're now listed as a missing person. I advise you to contact police headquarters in San Antonio as soon as possible. They will want a statement from you."

"Yes, I suppose that would be sensible of me. Thank you for bringing the matter to my attention."

A smile flickered on the officer's face. "No problem." The man turned toward his table then quickly swung back toward Chris. "My wife would be thrilled if I'd bring your autograph home." Color traced the edges of prominent ears poking out from his buzz-cut hairline.

"I'd be honored." Chris grinned wide. "Do you have anything for me to write on?"

"Sure." He pulled the ticket pad from his belt and ripped off a sheet.

Chris took the paper and raised an eyebrow. "Signing this isn't going to get me into any trouble, is it?"

"Naw. Write your name on the back. Best use of one of these things I've seen in a long while."

Seconds later, the officer strolled away, smiling and tucking the autographed page into the breast pocket of his shirt.

Chris stuck more than enough cash to cover the bill

into the discreet black folder the waitress had supplied, and then he stood up. "Shall we?"

Nursing reluctant admiration, Maddie followed him toward the exit. Chris Mason possessed a brand of courage she could only dream about. His occupation kept him in the public eye 24/7 and thrust him in front of a camera, speaking to millions of people at a time. She'd rather engage a squadron of enemy forces single-handed than give a speech.

They climbed into Ginger, and Maddie directed the car out of the parking lot with extra caution not to exhibit the fire under the old gal's hood. Next to her, Chris pecked and swiped at his smart phone.

"Evidently, we're not wanted for anything at the moment," she said, "or that encounter would have ended with us in handcuffs, not a publicity op. But news of your presence in Laredo will now spread to San Antonio as soon as that officer reports in."

"At least he didn't ask me to introduce you, or it would go viral that we're hanging out together."

Maddie chuckled. "Suits me fine that my chair might as well have been an empty seat for all the attention he paid me. Where to now?"

"Here's the location of the nearest library." He read off the directions.

Ten minutes later they had cruised a few miles up I-35 and were entering the main library on Carlton Road. Maddie inhaled the warm, woody, slightly sweet smell of books and bookshelves overlaid by air freshener. Chris proceeded at a brisk pace to the main counter, and Maddie trailed him, casing the area for potential threats and escape routes.

"Excuse me," Chris said to the man behind the counter. "I'm looking for a book entitled *A Grunt's War in Vietnam*. Do you have a copy?"

"Let me see." The librarian, whose name tag identified him as Phil, tapped a few keys on the computer keyboard, hummed, and then turned toward them. "Yes, we have a copy, but I'm sorry, it's checked out."

Maddie's gut tensed. At least Chris had the presence of mind not to show the librarian the half bookmark taken from the crime scene.

"Too bad." Chris leaned a forearm on the counter. "Can you tell me anything about the author?"

Phil poked a little more at his keyboard then his face lit up. "Well, what do you know…"

What? Maddie bit her lip against barking the question aloud.

"The author bio in our system says Hector Herrera was a native of Laredo. One of our hometown boys."

"Was?" Chris canted his head.

The smile died on Phil's face. "Says here his sister Bonita Herrera issued his memoir posthumously. I recognize the publisher. It's one of those self-publishing outfits, but reputable. Copyright date is just last year."

"Is the sister still a resident of Laredo?"

Phil showed empty hands. "No clue. Doesn't say. You doing research or something?"

"Research, definitely."

The librarian's eyes narrowed. "You look familiar. Have we met?"

"I have one of those faces people seem to recognize."

Phil pursed his lips and looked unconvinced, but he turned back toward his computer monitor. "Let me check our event archives for you. Since the author was a local, we may have hosted a book-launch party. In which case, the sister would most likely have been the presenter, and we would have contact information. I couldn't give out an address or phone number, but I could take yours and let her know a researcher is interested in talking to her."

"That would be great."

The clicking and scanning went on for some time. Maddie eased from one foot to the other. Were they on the verge of a breakthrough or a dead end? This research business was every bit that combination of tedium and tension that marked the countdown before an assault.

Phil let out a huff. "Sorry, we have no record of an event hosted by our library for that book release."

"Thanks for trying." Chris backed away from the desk.

"Welcome." The librarian's gaze drifted toward his computer monitor.

Maddie's stomach knotted as Chris took her elbow and led her into a maze of bookshelves. "What now?" Her words came out in a breathy whisper.

"We attack the problem from a different angle. Have a seat." He motioned toward a wingback chair in a reading alcove.

Maddie eased into it while Chris sat across from her and tapped and swiped on his cell phone, making little clicking noises with his tongue against his teeth that got on her last nerve. She twiddled her fingers against the faux-leather arm of the chair and then rose and paced. Shadows moved and air currents shifted faintly as patrons soft-footed through the area. She didn't like being trapped in a corner like this. They needed to move soon.

"Houston, we have liftoff." Chris chuckled.

"You found something?" Her tone was sharper than intended.

Chris's eyebrows arched as he rose. "Ms. Herrera has a website for the book, but the contact form goes to a blind mailbox. Not much help there. Plugging Bonita Herrera into a White Pages search for Laredo, Texas, offered similar bupkes. That didn't worry me too much. I figured she might be using her maiden name in connection with the book release, but then her White Pages listing would be under her married name."

"How did you get around that little detail? Sounds pretty hopeless to me."

Chris grinned. "I entered Hector Herrera."

"But he's dead."

"True enough, but I got a hit with that inquiry, and the family member in the sublisting is a woman by the name of Bonita Bates."

"The sister?"

"I'd be surprised if it wasn't."

"But why—"

Chris held up a quieting hand, and Maddie contained her impatience—barely.

"Evidently Hector's sister uses his name and number as her own telephone number. I surmise that she may have been widowed at some point and wound up living with her brother until his passing. Women living alone often retain their phone listing under the man of the household as a means of protection."

Maddie snorted. "Not much protection if you could expose her ploy with a few keystrokes. So much for personal privacy."

"It's largely an illusion in this electronic age."

"Not comforting with all the crazies out there."

Chris rolled his shoulders. "Makes you look higher than your own resources for a sense of safety."

"Tell that to my dead comrades in arms…and my brother, too." Maddie tasted the bitterness rolling off her tongue, but she couldn't stop the words.

Chris's steady gaze oozed sympathy. Maddie dropped her attention to the low-napped carpet beneath their feet.

"It's okay to be angry, Maddie. I'm angry, too."

She peered up at him. There was no judgment on his face. She sucked in a long, deep breath. "Let's keep hunting for justice. Okay? Maybe then I can..."

Maybe then she could what? Resolve her grief? Find peace? Forgive God? How clichéd was all of that?

"You shouldn't feel guilty because you survived. It wasn't your fault. Any of it."

Huh? Maddie blinked and froze.

Chris strode away between the shelving. She shook off her paralysis and scampered after him. The guy was going to get himself killed if he dropped verbal bombs on her and then pranced away from the protection of his unofficial bodyguard. She caught up with Chris, tugged his arm to slow him down, then passed him, gaze roving, assessing, marking potential threats and possible cover. They exited the library, and Maddie thumbed Ginger's remote start button. The Oldsmobile purred to life, and they walked over and climbed inside.

She glared toward her passenger. "So, Mr. Therapist, what makes you think I feel guilty for living?"

"Because I did—for months. My whole perception of reality and what's truly important shifted that night. Finally, I figured that for my survival to matter, I needed to expose the truth about what happened that night."

"The real truth? Not just whatever dirt you can scrounge that will shoot you up the celebrity ladder?"

Chris's blue gaze darkened, but he didn't look away from her charged stare. "The whole truth and nothing but the truth."

Maddie squelched a reluctant grin that tugged at the corners of her lips. "You're not on the witness stand, you know."

"But I feel like I'm on trial."

She looked away from him and headed Ginger out of the parking lot. "Which direction now?"

A heavy sigh let her know that her nonanswer had stung. Maddie's heart squeezed in her chest. He had no idea how much she wanted to believe him, and for that very reason, she needed to keep her guard up until the truth he was talking about became crystal clear to her.

Chris consulted his phone and rattled off directions to a neighborhood on the south side of the city very near the Rio Grande and the lawless bastion of drug runners—Nuevo Laredo, Mexico.

"Prime location for someone tied in with moving drugs," Chris said.

"No argument there. Maybe we're onto something after all."

A sensation like a feather brushing down her spine sent a shiver through her frame. Could she really hope they would find answers and win free of the threat that had dogged her steps for so long that carefree moments were bittersweet memories?

A half hour later they pulled up in front of a small brick bungalow fronted by a low, open porch. The house looked well kept, though the door and windows wore bars, and the yard was brown and dead.

"I'm going to introduce myself by name," Chris said. "It's a gamble, considering we're trying to avoid killers on our trail, but knowledge of my identity could produce a telltale reaction of guilt and fear… That is, if this Bonita Bates played a part in the betrayal."

Maddie nodded. "And if she didn't, a little name-dropping from someone who might publicize her book could get her to talk freely. Maybe she'll say something that will give us a lead. I think it's worth the risk."

Chris's answering grin shot tingles through her.

They got out of the car, and Maddie came around to stand on the cracked sidewalk beside Chris. The man stared at the house, then suddenly jerked and rocked back. Maddie gripped his arm. The muscles beneath her hand were rigid. She followed the line of his gaze toward the side of the house where a white-haired woman in a wheelchair rolled slowly down a long ramp toward them.

Then she looked up at Chris's drawn face. What did she see there? Guilt? Fear? Sorrow?

"Serena, I'm so sorry." The words pulsed from his lips, barely audible.

Who was Serena? Something nipped Maddie's insides. Jealousy? No way! But his reaction was guilt. Definitely. The emotion they'd been talking about less than an hour ago. What was it about this woman that raked raw shame to the surface of this man's iron composure?

The vise squeezing his arm brought Chris back to the present—away from the remembered flash and thunder of a single gunshot and the blood. So much precious blood. He glanced down. That was no vise. It was Maddie's white-knuckled grip around his biceps.

"What was that all about?" She took her hand away while he scrubbed his fingertips across his forehead and inhaled a deep breath.

"Bad memory. Sorry about that," he said.

"What—"

"Let's just say that the Rio isn't the only time a bullet has nearly taken me out."

Maddie's brow furrowed and her mouth opened, but Chris walked away from her toward the woman in the wheelchair, who had stopped at the bottom of the ramp to survey them with wary eyes. The dumpling-shaped woman dressed in a T-shirt and lightweight sweatpants really looked nothing like his petite, elegant Serena. It was just the wheelchair and the bone-white hair that had thrown him back in time. This person was old enough to warrant the snowy locks that frizzed around her head, not like the vibrant young woman with her whole life ahead of her who went white in a single day and landed in a wheelchair because he had trusted the wrong person. If he'd needed any reminder that his attraction to Maddie was a recipe for disaster, this was it.

"Hi, I'm Christopher Mason, a reporter from *World News*." He stopped in front of the woman's chair and extended his hand. "I'm interested in the memoir you published about your brother's experiences in Vietnam."

The sixtysomething woman's cautious expression melted into a smile, and she offered a weak but steady handshake. "*World News!* What do you know about that?"

Her gaze showed no alarm. Either Bonita Bates wasn't in on the conspiracy, or she was the uncrowned queen of subterfuge. Apparently, she hadn't seen the news reports of his near demise, either. No dark curiosity marred the delight on her face.

She slapped the arm of her wheelchair. "I was always after Hector to have that memoir published. He had a way with words, you know, and a big ax to grind about how that war was handled. But he insisted no one should see the baring of his soul until he was gone. Well, I took him seriously, and got the thing into print within a year after he passed. There's been a decent amount of attention paid. More than I thought might come of a book about events that happened decades ago."

"Congratulations." His peripheral vision caught Maddie easing into a position nearby, her gaze scanning the neighborhood. Chris kept his attention on the woman before him. "I don't think this country will ever forget those turbulent years. We'd be foolish if we did. I assume you must be Hector's sister, Bonita."

"That I am. And your lady friend?"

"This is my assistant."

If Maddie objected to being dubbed an assistant or if Bonita noticed he'd not supplied a name, neither of them batted an eyelash.

Hector's sister gestured with a welcoming hand. "Come on in and ask your questions, as long as you don't mind a bit of clutter. I've got some sweet tea in the fridge and supermarket cookies in the cupboard."

"You don't need to serve us anything, but I'd be interested in sitting down for a chat."

A few minutes later, Chris had pushed his hostess's chair into the house, and they were installed in a rather dim, musty front room surrounded by the promised clutter. Pathways for the wheelchair were about the only open spaces between bags and boxes of who knew what and stacks of newspapers and magazines.

Chris's gaze fell upon an 8 x 10 framed photo occupying the center of a dusty coffee table. The photo featured a wildly grinning younger version of Bonita standing upright beside a youthful, smiling man dressed in a military uniform. They were posed in front of the very house they now occupied.

He gestured toward the picture. "You and your brother?"

"Yes, that was us right before he shipped out. I found the photo in a box of memorabilia while I was preparing the memoir for publication. It gave me inspiration." The woman's gaze went wistful. "Those were better days. I was among the lucky ones that Hector came back from the war, but he was never the cheerful fellow he used to be. He ranted about the way the government played politics with G.I.'s lives, and worse, protected the rights of protesters who spat on servicemen."

"Did he do anything about it?" Chris asked.

A half smirk, half grimace passed over Bonita's face. "Sure did. He wrote enough letters to newspapers, congressmen and government agencies to fill a book. I included a few samples at the end of the memoirs. Guess he made enough noise, and maybe said the wrong things to the wrong people, that the FBI started harassing him... and us, too—my husband, Dane, and me."

She scowled. "I've always felt it was upset over the government persecution that made Dane jumpy behind the wheel the night we had the accident that killed him and put me in this." She patted the left wheel of her chair. "After that, I moved in with Hector in this home where we grew up. He was no picnic to live with, but I understood why."

"Tell me about the good days, and then the war."

Perched on the edge of a straight-backed chair opposite Chris, Maddie's lips pressed together. She probably figured he was wasting time. He sent her a quelling look, and her shoulders eased out of their rigid line.

For the next half hour, Bonita poured out her heart about growing up with her brother, then the war that changed him. Chris countered with gentle, prodding questions. Animation and genuineness flowed from her. If her story glossed over nefarious activities perpetrated by her brother or herself since Nam, Oscar awards should rain from the sky.

"Here I am telling you these things you already found out in the book," she said. "I haven't even asked you. What did you think of it?" Bonita folded her hands in front of her, and gazed at him with the air of an eager puppy.

Chris regarded her gravely. This was in no way the sort of person he'd expected to meet, and he couldn't stretch his imagination far enough to picture this disabled, elderly hoarder pulling the trigger that killed Agent Jackson. Judging by her handshake, she hadn't the strength to so much as raise the gun. But something about the bookmark in the agent's hand was significant enough to warrant him spending his last second of life ripping it in half.

He spread his palms. "To be honest with you, Bonita, I haven't read it yet. I found out about the book under rather stressful circumstances. When I asked for it in the library, it was checked out, so I came looking for you."

Bonita's eyes widened and her mouth opened, but no sound came out. Then she clamped her jaw shut and color drained from her face. Had his honest answer cost them a chance to lay hands on the book and any clues it might hold? He exchanged troubled glances with Maddie.

"I suppose I could spare a copy for publicity purposes." Bonita's words emerged between pursed lips.

"My network wouldn't dream of accepting a copy for a penny less than fair market value. In fact, we'll take a case."

"Really?" The woman blinked, and a flush worked its way up her neck. "That would be so nice. You could pass them around the newsroom or give them out to viewers to build interest. You could—" The babble of words stopped, and tears suddenly glistened on the older woman's eyelashes. "Oh, bother! It's no good pretending." Her gaze dropped toward the floor. "I haven't sold more than a handful of copies. The one in the library I donated. I'm surprised it was checked out. I spent the life insurance proceeds Hector left me on getting this book out through one of those vanity presses, thinking sales would provide me with steady income. I even ordered a bunch of copies for myself to direct sell. Now I'm stuck with cases of books, and not enough pension income to make ends meet each month." She sniffed. "Not that you needed to know my troubles."

Chris leaned back in his chair. That explained the boxes taking up every available inch of space. Not so much a hoarder then, but a victim of high hopes and poor judgment fueled by love. Another similarity Bonita shared with his Serena.

A movement drew his attention, and Maddie crossed his line of sight, then knelt beside the older woman and offered her a tissue. Chris's heart warmed. Sure, the ex-ranger was tough when she had to be, and prickly as a saguaro toward him, but a toasted marshmallow didn't ooze as much tenderness as she did right now.

"You did a good thing, honoring your brother," Maddie said.

"I did?" Bonita lifted her head.

"Of course. And I'm quite certain Chris will do whatever he can to get the word out about the book."

The older woman beamed, and they both lasered him with expectant gazes.

What could he say? "Yes, absolutely."

Bonita spurted a laugh and smacked the arm of her chair. "Then help yourself to one of these boxes lying around. You can make the check out to me." She named a price that ruffled the hair on the nape of his neck. "I'm giving you a break. That's my production cost per case, but it'll keep me in groceries this week."

"Will cash do?" Chris pulled out the money and slipped a couple of extra twenties among the bills.

Wearing a tiny smile, Maddie nodded toward him. She approved. Heat warmed Chris's cheeks. The woman noticed everything. A great characteristic in a bodyguard, but a little embarrassing if a guy wanted to indulge a little private kindness. How he could promote this overpriced, self-published memoir of suspect quality, he had no idea, but he'd figure something out. If he and Maddie lived long enough to return to normal lives.

"Here." Bonita held out a short stack of colorful lengths of cardstock. "You need bookmarks to go with your purchase. I give these out free. I designed them myself and had them printed locally." The statement emerged with a note of pride.

Printed locally?

Chris's pulse jumped as he accepted the bookmarks and noted the name of the print shop on the bottom of one. This information would have been on the half of the bookmark he had not taken from the crime scene—the half clutched in the dead man's fist. His gaze collided with Maddie's, and understanding arced between them.

On the way out to the car, lugging a case of books, he glanced at her. "Are you thinking what I'm thinking?"

She flashed a muted grin. "The clue isn't the book—it's the bookmark."

"You're not a bad Sherlock yourself."

She chuckled. "Next stop, a printing business in the heart of Laredo. Wonder if it will turn out to be a front for a nest of drug runners." She rubbed her hands together. "I'm starting to have hope for this line of investigation."

Chris's jaw tightened. Similar hope warred with dread that the lead could as easily peter out into nothing. He'd been in the investigative reporting business long enough to realize its frustrations. If the print shop proved to be a dead end, where did that leave them? Still hanging in the wind, targets for the next hired assassin who ran them down.

FIVE

The slightly dingy clapboard facade of the mom-and-pop printing store screamed innocence—maybe too loudly. Beneath an old-fashioned striped awning, a narrow white-washed door was bracketed between a pair of display windows where small stacks of brightly colored card stock and samples of stationery invited potential customers to step inside.

Maddie grabbed Chris's arm as he attempted to do just that. "Let me take point position. I'll feel more comfortable if I have a clear view of the perimeter without your back blocking my view."

Chris made a small exasperated noise. Maddie ignored his ill humor and moved ahead of him through the door. A bell over the lintel sounded, and the scent of ink greeted her, but no one occupied the front section of the shop. A scuffed wooden customer counter dominated the small space, front and center, while a ceiling-tall shelf loomed to the left, offering more stationery and cardstock. *Ka-thunk, ka-thunk* sounds carried to them through an open doorway behind the customer counter.

Chris came up beside Maddie, hands stuffed in his pants pockets. "Maybe the owner is out to lunch."

Maddie checked her watch. It was pushing noon. "With

the machinery running? I don't think so." She took a step toward the counter.

"Hold your horses. I'll be right out," a scratchy voice called from the interior of the building.

The rhythm of the machine slowed and then abruptly ceased. A thin, older man with a slight stoop in his walk emerged from the workroom, wiping his hands on a rag. His bibbed apron over denim pants and a button-down shirt reminded Maddie of a newspaperman's get-up from the old West. The scowl that deepened the wrinkles on his narrow face smoothed away at the sight of them.

He let out a small grunt. "Thought you were the paper-product sales guy. Usually shows up about this time."

"Not a welcome event, I take it?" Chris chuckled.

The printer lifted one side of his mouth in a half grimace, half smile. "I'm a dinosaur, and a lot of these products for newfangled contraptions confuse me. I should probably retire and sell the place, but I seem to have ink in my blood." He laid his rag on the countertop. "What can I do for you folks today?"

Chris held out one of the bookmarks. "I think you printed these."

"Let me see." The man plucked a pair of glasses from his shirt pocket and perched them on his sharp nose. He peered at the printed strip of cardstock. "Yep. 'Bout a year ago. Nice lady in a wheelchair. Do you like it? Are you interested in a similar job? I could set you up with—"

The jangle of the entry bell cut the man's words short. Maddie whirled and instinctively placed herself between the newcomer and Chris. Tension ebbed from her muscles. If the print-shop owner resembled a newspaperman from a B Western, the young man slouching through the door was nearly a dead ringer for a scruffy Marty McFly Jr. from *Back to the Future II*—minus the high-tech jacket. This late teen/early twentysomething wore a T-shirt that said, *Do Not Disturb. I'm Disturbed Enough Already.* Maybe she shouldn't have been so quick to relax.

The scowl reappeared on the shop man's face. "Figured you'd be by today."

"Like clockwork, y'know. Ready to serve your stationery needs." He smirked and waggled a thin catalog in his hand that featured a variety of paper and ink supplies on the cover.

The paper salesman's grin sent a shock wave down Maddie's spine. She'd seen warmer smiles on a bleached skull. Actually, the young man's face resembled a skull—sallow skin stretched tight across prominent bones. A fevered brightness glinted from his pale blue eyes. Not a healthy specimen. She exchanged glances with Chris, whose lips had thinned to a flat line.

"You want the usual order?" Ignoring Maddie and Chris, the salesman barged between them and slapped the catalog onto the counter.

The shop owner jerked at the whiplike sound, but he lifted his chin. "Business has been a little slow lately. I made out a list." He reached into a drawer beneath the counter and handed a slip of lined paper to the young man.

The salesman scanned the list and clicked his tongue. "People gotta pay their bills, y'know. Including me. I work on commission. What would happen if everybody cut their orders in half? I couldn't pay my rent, and I'd get evicted. You don't want that to happen, do ya?" He finished his little speech with a laugh. Not a nice one.

Maddie's teeth gritted together. This kid might look a little like a sickly Marty McFly, but he was the half-wit bully Biff in an undersize body. Chris cleared his throat, and the young salesman shot him a glance then transferred his attention to Maddie.

"What are you lookin' at?" he said. "Don't you have some shopping to do so this hardworking printer can stay busy?"

The guy was nuts. Certifiable. And on something that made him potentially dangerous.

Maddie scooped up the sales catalog and rolled it into a tight baton. "Don't you have an order to fill?"

The salesman jutted his jaw and met Maddie's glare. She tapped the catalog baton in the palm of her other hand. Her peripheral vision noted Chris move in closer. If this kid didn't back down, he was going to get clobbered from two sides.

"On second thought," the shop owner burst out, "I'll take the usual order."

"Buy more supplies than you can use?" Chris said. "I don't think so. No salesman in his right mind wants his customers overstocked. That would cut into future orders and impact the profitability of his employer and the businesses he services."

A tremor shivered the salesman's too-lean body, and he blinked those reptilian eyes at Maddie, then turned toward Chris. A full head taller, shoulders squared, Chris smiled down at the younger man and settled a fist on the countertop. Maddie allowed herself in inner smirk. The TV newsman might not be a soldier, but he had savvy and spine to go along with his smarts.

The belligerence faded from the salesman's stance. "Yeah, sure." He shrugged. "I'll go get the stuff out of the truck. Leave it on the pallet out back like usual?" He jerked his chin toward the shop owner.

The businessman offered a trembly smile. "That would be fine. The door is already open because I knew you'd be by any minute."

The young man slouched outside, three pairs of eyes following him.

Chris turned toward the printer. "I assume you purchased the card stock for the bookmark from the company represented by our departed salesman."

"Indeed, I did. They pretty much have a corner on the paper business in our area. Their prices are decent, but the turnover rate in sales reps is ridiculous. I never know who is going to show up, and I usually don't like them. Maybe they don't pay well enough to attract a better quality of employee, and that's why their prices stay reasonable."

Chris let out a soft hum. "You could be right about that."

Small sounds drifted from the back of the shop. Maddie met Chris's gaze, and he tilted his head the slightest degree in that direction. She swallowed a smile. Time to supervise a delivery.

Chris motioned toward the businessman. "Why don't you show me some more of your stationery options? I see some I like."

The printer grinned as he came around the counter and joined Chris in front of the display shelf. Maddie glided into the back room and passed between several pieces of equipment. Most of the machines looked as if they came from a bygone era, though traces of fresh ink and partially finished projects attested that they were still in use. A few of the more compact machines were from the current digital age. Despite his comment about being a "dinosaur," the shop owner must be trying to educate himself on new technology.

At the rear of the workroom, the Biff-McFly salesman had propped the back door open and was carrying cases of products from a van into the shop. Head down, he was muttering to himself and gave no sign that he noticed Maddie as she took up an observation post in a shadow near a sorting counter. Crackhead if she'd ever seen one.

What kind of business hired dopers on a regular basis? One linked with the drug trade? Her gaze found the name on the outside of a box. *Rio Grande Paper Supply.* Chris ought to be able to get an address and directions to the place from his smart phone.

The salesman set a small stack of boxes labeled Toner on top of a larger stack of paper cases, then dusted his hands together. His gaze zeroed in on one of the newer pieces of equipment and a smirk formed on his face. Darting a glance toward the front of the store, where Chris's voice alternated with the printer's, he scooted to the machine and reached toward it. Maddie cleared her throat. The young man jerked and stared around, gaze finally alighting on her. His mouth fell open.

"Nice day, isn't it?" she said. Unless she missed her guess, the shop owner would have found that piece of equipment sabotaged when he returned to work back here.

"Um, yeah." The would-be vandal's head went down, and he hustled out the door. His vehicle departed with a screech of tires.

Shaking her head, Maddie kicked the doorstop away from the rear exit and closed and locked the door, then returned to the front of the building. The printer shot her a startled glance as she joined him and Chris, but didn't pause in ringing up the total for a box of stationery lying on the counter.

Moments later, she and Chris exited the store and climbed into Ginger.

"Rio Grande Paper Supply," she said.

"Roger that," he responded and pulled out his phone.

Maddie chuckled. "There's hope yet that you'll get army-trained."

Chris grinned. "And you are about to take a major new step in your investigative training."

She awarded him a questioning look.

"Stakeout, here we come."

"I thought only cops did that stuff."

"You have much to learn, Grasshopper. Much to learn. First stop, a grocery store to stock up on food and beverages. Surveillance can be hungry, thirsty work."

"And boring."

"That, too."

"But not too boring, I hope. This needs to be a breakthrough."

"I concur."

Maddie pulled the Oldsmobile into traffic, gnawing gently on one edge of her lower lip. It was amazing—and a little weird and scary—how the two of them worked together like they'd known each other for life. A look…a nod…and they each seemed to know what the other was thinking. A friend of hers once told her such intuitive communication happened between old married couples or budding soul mates. *Whoa!* Did this mean her heart was in danger of being captured by a traitor to his country?

She couldn't allow that. Whatever it took, she'd keep a close guard on her feelings.

Now what was bugging this prickly woman? Chris had thought they were starting to forge a bond, maybe get past some of the suspicion, but she'd gone stiff and silent while they shopped for supplies. Then they'd scouted out the location of the paper-manufacturing plant on the outskirts of the city and found a promising perch in the shade of some bushes on a boulder-strewn ridge above the sprawling factory. All the while, she'd shared scarcely a word with him. Now she sat cross-legged beside him on the ground, crunching an apple, gaze fixed on the activity—or lack thereof—below, as if he didn't exist.

Maybe it was time to clear the air and talk about some things that stomped around both their psyches like the elephant that refused to be ignored one second longer. Would she answer a few questions if he prodded a bit? One way to find out. He opened his mouth.

"Location, location, location." The statement popped from her lips and bridled Chris's tongue. "Look at the setup down there." She gestured with the core of her apple. "Main plant half the size of a football field. Warehouse half again that size and a fleet of semis backed up to assorted bays. Not to mention the vans handling local business. All located less than a mile from the Rio Grande and surrounded by gullies and washes offering perfect cover for the importation of drugs by mule-back. I think we've struck gold here. Now we just need something concrete to verify our suspicions."

Chris lifted their newly purchased binoculars to his eyes. The sprawling parking lot and front entrance of the factory snapped into close view. "Pretty quiet down there. Minor comings and goings, but normal for a business this size. I suppose we'll see mass exodus at quitting time. If anything hinky is going to take place, it will likely happen after dark."

"Roger that. I'm going to take a siesta." Maddie settled back against a rock and closed her eyes.

"So what *do* you remember?"

Her eyes popped open. "About what?"

"You know. The night of the attack."

A long sigh hissed between her lips, and her back straightened. "Do we need to talk about this now?"

"If not now, then when?"

"I don't know." Maddie drew her legs up to her chest.

Silence fell, but she didn't lapse into her napping pose. Chris waited for her decision to talk…or not.

"I was standing at the river's edge, watching moonlight play spooky games on the water," she said at last. "And thinking about…things."

Her gaze pierced him as if he should know what things she meant. Something that involved him?

Her gaze dropped, and she picked up a stick and began drawing squiggles in the dirt around her feet. "You know. Sorting out some feelings and getting my mind straight for the assault the next day. That's where I was when the first mortar round hit the camp. If I'd been in my tent where I belonged—where my com equipment was set up—I could have sent out the call for help. Maybe I could even have gotten Lorraine out." Her voice choked off. She was referring to her tent mate, DEA agent Lorraine Hitchins, also numbered among the dead. Maddie cleared her throat. "As it was, I had to run back toward my tent, and then suddenly I was blown off my feet, and everything went black. *Finito!* That's the extent of my memories."

Sights, sounds, smells from that night flooded Chris's senses, and he inhaled sharply against the wrenching memory. In his mind's eye, the first blast illuminated the camp like daylight. Several tents, including his, where his cameraman had been asleep on a cot, were obliterated in a stink of sulfur and smoke. In that moment, Chris's heart had attempted to jackhammer a hole in his chest, but he'd stood frozen. Combat-trained Maddie had raced past him, not knowing his presence in the dark.

"If you had been in your tent," he said, "you'd be dead along with Lorraine. Yours was the next to go. You wouldn't have had time to send your distress signal."

Her gaze narrowed on him. "You're sure about that?"

"Positive."

Her expression brightened then went dark. "Makes no difference. I was still away from my post. Where were *you* when the attack started?"

The wattage of her glare let Chris know this question burned in her heart. What could he tell her without treading on territory where he dared not go?

"I wasn't in my tent, either."

Her nostrils flared. "Why not?"

"Couldn't sleep." He shrugged. Did she see through his nonchalance?

She frowned but said nothing. Clearly, he needed to elaborate or risk deepening her mistrust of him. But there was no way he could confess he wasn't in his tent because he was watching her from the shadows and fighting a desire to draw close and gamble his heart on a stolen a kiss.

"I was keyed up about what the next day might bring," he said. "I was drawn to the river, too. In fact, I saw you there and might have made my presence known but then the attack started. You reacted instantly, but it took me a second or two to shake off my disbelief. Then I was yards behind you in racing into camp. The next barrage hit, taking out the com tent, among other things, and you flew into the air and landed almost at my feet. I thought you were dead."

His voice cracked on the final word, and he cleared his throat. Even now, recalling that instant in time struck him nearly dumb with his heart in his throat—not because he had stood so near to danger, but because he'd nearly lost Maddie. How pathetic was the intensity of his fear of losing her when he couldn't risk telling her how much he cared?

Her wide eyes devoured him. He could almost see the wheels of thought turning in her head. "What did you do next?"

"Are you going to believe me if I tell you?"

She pursed her lips then jerked a tiny nod. "Let's assume that."

Chris inhaled a deep breath, like a swimmer about to take a plunge. "I'm aware that it's not recommended to move an injured person before professional help arrives, but we were both in danger of being obliterated at any second if we stayed where we were. So I picked you up and took off into the desert, away from the attack zone."

Maddie's jaw dropped. "That's how I ended up several hundred yards away from the destroyed camp when the rescuers found me."

"Bingo."

"But the report said I was lying unattended when they recovered me. Where did you go?"

"To get help, but the first unit I encountered bundled me away willy-nilly. I never saw you again. They wouldn't even let me visit you in the military hospital."

"You tried to visit me?"

"I sent flowers and a card. Didn't you get them?"

"Negative. I suspect the investigators weren't into allowing contact between the survivors while they were looking into the catastrophe and assigning blame in the most face-saving way possible for the bigwigs." She stopped speaking with her mouth open, like she was searching for her next words. Her gaze slid away from his. "Thanks for saving my life, by the way."

Chris's heart leaped. "So you do believe me?"

"Let's just say that this information fills a gap in my understanding of events in a fairly plausible manner."

A sour taste coated Chris's tongue. What had he expected? Instant warmth and new best-friend status? Her walls of self-defense had been up too long for a brief conversation to tear them down. Maybe he'd chipped away at the bricks a bit, but he'd be a fool to push her shaky trust level by offering the rest of his story. Even he could hardly believe that part.

"I'm going to grab that siesta," she said.

He grunted and put the binoculars to his eyes. Probably a waste of time to look for suspicious activity in broad daylight. Maybe he should follow Maddie's lead and indulge in a little shut-eye. The next hours passed in fitful snoozing, stretching their legs and snacking on their provisions. At last, quitting time arrived for the employees, the parking lot emptied, and darkness wrapped an inky fist around the area. The moon and stars were apparently taking a snooze beneath a cloud-cover blanket.

A few pinpricks of light above entrances and loading docks offered markers for a single uniformed security guard who made the rounds once and then twice before midnight. Chris's spirits fell. Rumors of his nosy presence should have rattled enough cages to produce some kind of response if this was a drug distribution depot, but there was no hint of clandestine activity at this location.

"Why is a light still on in a second-floor office?" Maddie asked in his ear.

"Security guard station?"

"Not on the second floor."

"You tell me then."

She chuckled. "Someone's working late, or they're waiting for an after-hours visitor."

Headlights appeared on the road leading up to the factory. A car pulled into the parking lot, and a dark figure emerged—a man, judging from size and build, but it was too dark to see his features even with the binoculars. Chris followed the man's stride toward the front door anyway. The security guard opened the entrance from the inside, and the midnight visitor passed beneath the overhead light. Just before he went inside, the man glanced over his shoulder, presenting a three-quarter profile in the binocular's lens. Chris sucked air between his teeth.

"What?" Maddie's stage whisper broadcast impatience.

He lowered the binoculars. "Why would DEA Agent Clyde Ramsey visit a paper plant in the middle of the night?"

SIX

Out of the darkness, Chris's teeth gleamed a faint white in a grin that Maddie answered. "Guess I'll have to slip inside and find out," she said.

"You? Try *we*."

"Get real, Mason. Where did you receive reconnaissance training?"

"I have a doctorate in Snoopology. I'll let you 'take point,' as you like to say, but I'm glued to your heels."

"All right, but you're going to have to help out first by creating a distraction for the security guard."

"Whatever you say, but no ditching me once you're in."

"Deal."

"I suppose you have a plan?"

Maddie let out a soft snort. "What else have I had to do so far but play around with possibilities and contingencies in my mind? Dollars will get you donuts that those delivery vans in the parking lot are programmed for antitheft. What do you think the lone security guard will do if several of them sound off at once?"

"Step out to investigate."

"Precisely. One thing I've noted about those front doors as people go in and out—they're slow to close. We're going to use that knowledge to our advantage."

She leaned toward Chris and began to outline the rest of her plan. Concentration on the business at hand was easier said than done with the subtle scent of his masculine aftershave teasing her nostrils and sending warm tingles to her fingers and toes. Maddie mentally kicked herself. This was no time to toy with visions of his lips on hers the way she'd been doing that night along the Rio before the attack started. She was pathetic. Time to get some action going so this doomed attraction didn't run off with her good sense.

A half hour later, Chris had disappeared somewhere in the midst of the fleet of delivery vans, and Maddie stood with her back to the cool brick of the factory wall around the corner from the front entrance. She waited, breathing slow and even. Flashing lights and the screech of an alarm suddenly filled the air. First one van and then another and another sounded off.

A slight shiver ran through her. *Good job, Chris, but don't get carried away.*

Near at hand, the growl of a man's voice reached her ears, purpling the air about those blankety-blank raccoons. Maddie chanced a peek around the corner of the building. The guard was already several strides across the parking lot, gun drawn and gaze fixed at the far end where the vans were parked. The door gaped open but it was closing faster than she had anticipated. She dashed on cotton feet and snatched the door handle a nanosecond before it would have clicked shut.

Heart pounding, she let herself in and went at once to the security station in the rather sterile reception area. Her gaze scanned the equipment and settings. Good. The guard had left his computer portal open.

She sat down and quickly deleted the segment of camera footage that showed her entrance into the building and then turned off the recording capabilities altogether so she and Chris could move freely without leaving behind proof of their presence. She did a rapid check for internal-motion sensors and didn't find any, but that didn't mean there were none. She had no time to dig deeper into the system. In another few clicks she deactivated the entrance/exit alarms for the maximum period of ten minutes that the night-guard program allowed. They might have to escape the place from the roof. Good thing she had rope in her backpack.

The clamor from the parking lot diminished and then ceased. The guard would be heading back toward his station. She'd heard no gunfire and took that to mean he hadn't spotted Christopher Raccoon. A little grin formed on her face at the image of Chris with paws and fur and a burglar mask across his face. The guy was too cute for her peace of mind, even as a critter.

Her fingers danced a salsa across the keyboard. She only had seconds now. Could she finish her business? *Come on, fingers, move! There!*

She leaped up from the guard's chair and scurried down a dim hallway out of the guard's line of sight. Her last-instant chore had programmed the surveillance video of the past hour to rerun on the guard's monitors. If she and Chris hadn't finished their business and exited the building within that time, the cameras would go live, and the raccoon-hunting guard would have bigger game in his sights. Chris had better be Johnny-on-the-spot waiting for her to let him in at the door she'd designated. They were on the clock.

Ahead, a doorway loomed. A small night light revealed the words *Production Plant—Employees Only*. Maddie glided past an employee time clock and entered the plant. A sickly sweet smell greeted her, overlaid by a faint sulfurous tang. She wrinkled her nose. The reddish glow from a number of exit lights around the perimeter cast an eerie ambiance across the vast area populated by shadow monsters of massive equipment. Most of Cowboys Stadium would fit into the place.

A faint beam of whitish light streaming from above and to her left drew her attention. The second-floor offices had windows overlooking the plant, including the one that was lit, but the curtains were drawn, allowing only a sliver of illumination to escape. Good for Chris and her. The occupants of the office wouldn't be able to spot movement in the plant area.

In a cautious trot, Maddie skittered around equipment toward the first metal fire-escape door. She cracked it open and hissed into the warm darkness. A flash of distant lightning followed by a mutter of thunder answered her. The scent of moisture drifted on the breeze, and the electric air stirred hairs on her arms. Storm on the way. Where was Chris? She poked her head outside, and caught the movement of a shadow near a door farther down the outside wall.

"Over here," she whisper-called.

The shadow approached and morphed into Chris. He slipped inside, chuckling softly.

"That was the most fun I've had in a long time," he said in a soft rush of words. "The coons must drive the night help nuts around here on a regular basis. I've never heard a varmint called so many creative names."

"You do know the guard had a gun."

"Do I look like a raccoon to you?"

Maddie's mental Christopher Raccoon image resurfaced, and she swallowed a spurt of laughter. "I'm not sure the guy would have waited to discover the difference if he'd spotted movement out there."

"Point taken."

Maddie pressed a finger over her mouth and motioned for Chris to follow her toward a set of stairs that led to a door several windows down from the target office. They crept upward on snail time. Maddie winced at every creak and groan of the metal stairs, but the small sounds brought no response from whoever was meeting in the lit-up office. The door hinges could have used a squirt of oil, but at last they stood in a dim, carpeted hallway scented with air freshener that failed to totally mask the pungent odors from the paper-processing plant.

They crept closer to the office where light peeped from beneath the door. The sound of voices grew louder, but words were indistinct. Maddie noted a stairway from the other direction that likely led down to the reception area where the guard lurked. The stairs they had just used were metal and steep and offered no cover should they be pursued. Not a good scenario if they needed to vamoose suddenly. The skin on the back of her neck crawled, but she ignored the sensation. If they never took chances they'd never uncover the truth.

Please, God, let this midnight meeting shine a spotlight on the guilty parties.

Maddie took a few more steps forward, then the next step began to creak beneath her feet, and she froze. Chris brushed up against her, and his warm breath feathered through her hair, cascading tingles through her. She dismissed the sensation as she edged toward the other side of the hall and then proceeded forward. The voices were becoming more distinct. Agent Ramsey's she recognized. Two others belonged to strangers.

A click sounded behind her, and she whirled in combat stance. Chris jumped back, mouth agape. In one hand, he held a small recorder. Tension ebbed from Maddie's muscles, and she eased to her full height, scowling and shaking her head. Chris held his recorder toward the conversation that began to become clear in bits and snatches.

"...dangerous to move the stuff now." Agent Ramsey's gravel tones reached them.

A calmer voice replied, but only snatches were intelligible. There was something familiar about the man's polished tone and cadence, but Maddie couldn't figure out what.

"If we don't fulfill our end of the bargain in full and on time—" the man's volume rose "—Fernando will be very disappointed, and we can't risk that."

Maddie's ears perked up. Fernando? As in Fernando Ortiz, the leader of the Ortiz Drug Cartel, the ruthless thug who took credit for the Rio Grande Massacre and thumbed his nose at any authority trying to stop him from pursuing his evil business?

"...don't like it," inserted Agent Ramsey. "...nosy reporter at my door..."

"The issue is being addressed," a deep, bull voice pronounced. No problem hearing what this guy said.

"Your way of *addressing* the issue hasn't worked well so far." Ramsey's tone took on heightened clarity. "They're still alive."

"You're spooked over shadows," said the man with the bull voice. "We need to make our move when the cops are distracted and run ragged. We're not canceling the shipment."

Maddie met Chris's gaze, and he mouthed *shipment*. She nodded.

The calmer voice began to speak again, but little could be understood. Maddie allowed Chris to edge past her, recorder extended. She made out a few tidbits wafting from inside the office. Something about "midnight," "golden opportunity" and "fourth." Fourth what?

Chris took a baby step forward, then began another. Maddie suddenly spotted tell-tale pinpricks of red light embedded in the walls directly ahead of them, and her heart seized. Laser motion detectors. She grabbed for Chris to halt him in his tracks.

Too late!

The shriek of an alarm yanked Chris's heart to a halt. A hand in his collar whirled him and shoved him up the hall in the direction they'd come. His pulse went into overdrive and hot blood flooded his extremities. He dashed toward that second set of stairs they'd passed, but a shove sent him onward toward the stairs they'd come up.

"Not into the waiting arms of that trigger-happy guard!" Maddie's yell carried to him faintly above the alarm.

A bee-sound buzzed past his ear and something jerked at his hair. Great! Someone coming out of the office was armed, too, and he and Maddie were fish in a barrel in this hallway. He ducked low, scuttling along. At least it was semidark out here. His recorder shattered in his hand and a burning sensation traveled up his arm. No time to check if the bullet had drawn blood. He hit the door with his shoulder and held it for Maddie to charge through.

"Go! Go!" She punched his arm. "Hide among the equipment, then escape through the first door you can."

Chris hesitated, and she slugged him again. "No time for chivalry. You'll get us both killed."

He turned and took the stairs two at a time. If he missed his footing it would be a broken leg or a broken neck. Neither much mattered if a bullet found a vital organ. He reached the bottom of the stairs and turned to find the door at the top bursting open and Maddie only halfway down. He shouted a warning that she probably couldn't hear, but whether she heard him or was hyperaware of what was happening around her, she suddenly vaulted over the stair rail, hit the concrete floor and rolled.

Another *zing* near his ear sent Chris dashing behind the nearest piece of equipment. A bullet spanged off metal behind him, and he began a crouching zigzag pattern from the cover of one machine to another. The fingers of the hand that had held the recorder tingled as if they'd been asleep, but there was no time to stop and check the damage. His pulse roared in his ears louder than the shriek of the alarm.

Was Maddie all right? He deserved the Idiot Prize for hunting her down and getting her involved in this investigation. He should have pursued the leads on his own and caught the culprits. Then she'd be safe, not dodging bullets. *Yeah, right!* Without her, he'd be worm food already.

God, this is Chris with a major SOS!

Light showered down from above and the clangor ceased. Chris froze, clapping a hand over his eyes. Had he been hit by a bullet and sent to his reward? He hadn't felt any pain. Silent seconds ticked past. Slowly, he peeled his hand away from his face and blinked. Nope, he was not dead. He stood beside a mammoth piece of equipment resembling a giant giraffe. He checked the hand that tingled. No blood. The bullet hadn't ravaged flesh, only electronics.

Where was everyone? A shuffling sound came from his right rear flank, and another small noise wafted from his left. The skin on his entire body prickled. He was being stalked. Maddie had told him to find a door. He gazed around. No exit in sight. He was deep in the maze of machinery. On the far side of the plant, one of the pieces of equipment sputtered to life.

Maddie?

Smart girl. By the time the hunters reached that spot, she'd be long gone. Chris grinned. Two could play that game. He flipped the on switch of the giant giraffe and darted away as it clanged and clattered into motion. A man-shaped shadow on his right sent him crouching into cover behind a box-laden conveyor belt. He peered through the sliver of space between a pair of boxes and barely stopped himself from sucking in an audible breath.

Agent Ramsey stood, armed and dangerous, hard gaze flitting this way and that. *I'm not dirty,* the guy had claimed from the sanctity of his home. *Hah!* No slimier than a pig in a wallow. Someone needed to take this guy down. Hard. And he meant to do it, but not with a bullet. The right words reported to the right people would send this traitor to the penitentiary forever and a day.

But first he had to get out of here alive with Maddie by his side.

The agent shuffled off in a direction away from Chris's hiding place. Warm weakness threatened to collapse his legs beneath him, but he firmed his knees and moved on. His heart battered his ribs, and his mouth was dry as a baked stone. Did soldiers feel this way in the combat zone, or was he hopelessly civilian? The question was moot if he didn't find an exit…soon!

Ssst!

The faint hiss halted him. He gazed around and spotted a feminine hand poking from behind a piece of machinery. The forefinger beckoned him. Searching right and left for any sign of their deadly stalkers, he soft-footed toward her. He rounded the corner of the machine, and their gazes locked.

A sensation swept through him as if he were standing beneath the cascade of a sun-warmed fountain. Relief? Thanksgiving? Love? He batted that last absurd thought away. Maddie was alive and unharmed, and for the moment, nothing else mattered. Was he fooling himself to

think he saw a reflection of his sudden irrational burst of
joy in her eyes? What *did* they feel for each other? Would
they ever be able to talk about it? Not now, that was for
sure.

She placed a finger to her lips and pointed toward the
inside wall. Why would they move away from the exits?
He lifted his eyebrows. She mouthed *Trust me,* and he did.
More than he'd trusted another living soul—other than
his family—since a traitorous woman fired a bullet that
shattered his world. Ironic, since Maddie was the one who
harbored trust issues toward *him*.

Chris followed Maddie's lead to the edge of a line of
equipment. About six yards of open space separated them
from a doorway that led deeper into the building, probably into a cargo bay. Could they escape from there? She
must think so.

Head swiveling right to left, Maddie peered around their
meager cover. She lifted a hand and waved him on. Chris
charged across the open space, yanked the door open and
held it for her. A scowl was his reward for chivalry as she
darted from cover toward him.

From near at hand, the night guard's voice shouted an
obscenity. The guy sure had a limited vocabulary. A sharp
report sounded, and Maddie staggered as she all but fell
through the open door. Chris scrambled into the darkness
after her. The rasp of Maddie's breathing led him to her.
Blackness was nearly absolute in this area smelling of oil
and gasoline. He reached out to wrap her in his arms, but
instead her hand grabbed his shirt and dragged him up
against the wall beside her.

"Are you hit?" he rasped.

"Negative," she whispered back. "The bullet ripped
through my backpack though, and it's in tough shape.
Good thing my flashlight didn't fall out."

"Who cares about a backpack or a flashlight when—"

"Shh."

Chris clamped his jaw shut. Aggravating, bossy woman, but silence was the better part of wisdom at the moment.

The door began to open, and a hand bearing a gun poked inside. Maddie's arm swept down and something long and metallic connected with the gun, yanking it from its owner's grip and earning a howl as the injured gun hand was jerked back. She slammed the door and leaned against it. A bright beam shot from the flashlight she'd used to disarm the guard.

"There!" She pointed toward a straight-backed chair farther up the wall.

Chris scrambled to retrieve it for her, and she jammed the back of the chair under the doorknob.

"He'll have reinforcements soon," she said, "and they'll come at us from another direction, so we'd better scram quick, fast and in a hurry."

"Gotcha."

She scooped up the guard's gun while sweeping the beam of her flashlight through a mechanic shop that would be the envy of a lot of guys Chris knew. Neat and complete, except for a partially disassembled riding lawn mower sitting in the middle of the cement floor.

"There!" He pointed toward a door across the room.

Angry voices began to carry to them from the mammoth plant they'd escaped.

"Come on," Maddie said and headed toward their new escape route.

Chris trotted after her. She flung open the door, and they found themselves not outside, but entering a cavernous garage, populated by a couple of trucks and a van, in various stages of repair.

"This place is way too self-sufficient," he muttered.

"Yeah," Maddie agreed. "Makes you wonder why they don't want an outside shop working on their vehicles."

"Not if they're using them to transport drugs. This setup would be ideal, not only to maintain their own transportation fleet but to provide privacy to tuck contraband into secret compartments."

Brilliant light flashed through a bank of windows high in one wall, followed almost instantly by a boom of thunder.

"Let's go!" she cried. "The storm will give us cover."

Maddie took off toward a door at the rear of the garage, and Chris stayed on her heels. They plunged outside into wind-lashed gloom that swallowed the beam of the flashlight within a few feet of its source. The scent of ozone hung in the air like doom's signature. The hairs on the nape of Chris's neck prickled, but the possibility of being struck by lightning was less daunting than waiting for the certainty of being struck by a bullet.

Together, they left the meager protection of the building's overhang and raced toward a brief line of trees that clawed the night with writhing branches. Lightning slashed the sky once more, and a drumroll of thunder brought down a curtain of rain. One moment Chris was dry; the next he was soaked to the skin. Keeping Maddie in sight became almost impossible, even with the paltry beam of her flashlight to guide him.

Past the line of trees, they left the manicured lawn of the factory and entered a wilderness of rocks and cholla that set him stumbling and fighting for balance with every other step. They went on and on through the driving wet. He had no clue what direction they were headed in, or even if they weren't traipsing in circles. At least there was no chance of their hunters spotting them in this murk.

Water cascaded off his head and invaded his mouth,

his nose, his eyes. Forging onward became like trying not to drown while walking on land. Then the land ceased.

Chris plunged downward as if he'd stepped off the end of the earth. Abruptly, his fall ended, and his feet struck terra firma—or more like terra mucka. Bright pain spiked up his left leg, and his limbs buckled beneath him. He sprawled facedown and tasted bitter silt.

Lucky him. He'd found one of the ravines surrounding the paper plant. The chilly water pooling around him was attempting to drown him for real. Numbness invaded his body. He had no idea if he could move a muscle to escape the rising tide.

SEVEN

Maddie sensed Chris's sudden absence from her six, where he'd been practically breathing down her neck. She halted and scanned the few feet the flashlight's beam managed to illuminate in this wild weather. The wind drove rain straight into her face, and continuous flashes of lightning blinded rather than helped her to see. She'd been drier and seen more clearly during a night scuba-dive insertion in the Middle East. She squinted to make out the area a foot or two ahead.

There! Was that the lip of a ravine?

She crept forward and the beam of her light traveled down the side of a sheer drop, but didn't have the power to reach the bottom of the narrow cut in the earth. Chris had to be down there, but good luck hearing calls for help over the whoosh of falling rain and all-but-constant booms of thunder. She shrugged out of her pack and rummaged inside it through the gaping hole the bullet had torn in the canvas. Where was that nylon rope? If it had fallen out somewhere along their route, they were toast.

Her fingers closed on her quarry. Finally! Maddie pulled the cord from her pack, and her heart hit her toes. The bullet had taken a bite out of the rope along one of the folds and effectively left her with two parts. Would she have enough length to reach Chris? No matter. She had to try.

A tree stood nearby, old, gnarled and half dead, but it would serve to anchor one end of the rope so she could shimmy down and see if Chris was all right. He could have broken his neck. Or he could be lying down there unconscious, drowning in the water pooling at the bottom of the draw. Her heart seized like an engine that had exhausted its oil. No! She couldn't think like that and had no time to examine why the idea of him being hurt—or worse—filled her with panic.

Blanking her mind of all but the task at hand, she fastened one end of her abbreviated rope around the tree trunk then quickly tied knots for handholds down the remaining length. Even with the knots it was going to be a trick to hang on to the cord in this deluge.

She went to the edge of the ravine and began to let herself down. *I'm coming, Chris. Hang on! God, please help him.* The prayer wafted from her thoughts as naturally as prayer used to be for her. Nothing like a crisis to jumpstart faith. Or was it love for the man at the bottom? Why did her thoughts keep straying in that ridiculous direction? *Stay on task, woman!*

Her body slipped and slithered down the mud and rocks. No telling how many bruises she'd have to show for this stunt. *Rats!* She hung by the last knot in her rope, fibers digging into her palms, and her feet couldn't yet touch bottom. Climbing back up would mean leaving Chris to his fate, but letting go meant potential injury, or at the least, joining him in a trap with no known means of escape.

There was no decision to make.

She released her hold on the rope and tumbled downward. The drop was short. Slimy earth grabbed her feet, and she flexed her knees to absorb the impact.

"Chris!" Her voice sounded hollow in her ears, as if the wall of rain bounced the word back at her.

Maddie swiveled her head from side to side, straining into the murk for any sign of her companion. Was the raining letting up? Her visibility was becoming marginally clearer, the sting of raindrops less punishing, and lightning less frequent. She rummaged in her pack and retrieved the flashlight. The gun she'd taken from the security guard was gone—lost during her climb down the sheer wall. Small loss at the moment. She clicked the light on. Yes, the deluge was tapering off. The light beam reached farther than it had less than five minutes ago.

Where was Chris? Was she mistaken about what had happened? Had he disappeared into the night in some other direction and not fallen into the ravine at all? She couldn't have descended into this pit for nothing. Her stomach knotted. Why did she keep denying how much that pesky, persistent, lethally adorable reporter meant to her? A hand grabbed her elbow from behind. Maddie shrieked and whirled, bumping up against a slimy but solid chest.

"Chris?" The amazed gasp of his name escaped her as she gazed up into his storm-shadowed features.

His arms swallowed her, and she went into them, heart leaping like a joy-struck hare. Lips met lips, rain-chilled at first, then warm and firm and gentle and demanding all at once. For all she cared, this moment could last forever. But he pulled his face away, though he didn't unwrap his arms from around her.

"Let's get out of this rain," he said.

"Get out—"

She didn't finish the question as he took her by the hand and pulled her with a lurching stride toward a hollow in the side of the ravine that sat a good foot above the sodden bottom. Under the revealing beam of her flashlight, the area proved to be a tiny cave. They had to squat to sit under the cover of the low roof, but the niche provided a haven from the downpour on their heads. The floor of the cave was damp, though nothing like the inches of sucking mud at the bottom of the ravine.

"You're limping," she said.

"Not sure if my ankle is broken or just sprained."

"At least it wasn't your neck." She looked toward him.

His face hovered close…then closer…closer. Warm breath fanned her face. Her lips tingled, and her eyelids drooped. Another stolen kiss would taste so sweet. She shouldn't allow the caress, but she couldn't make herself stop him. Why live in reality when the fantasy of love spread balm across her stricken heart? She leaned forward a fraction of an inch and tasted…air.

He had turned his head and eased his body marginally away from hers. A sensation like shattering glass struck the pit of her stomach. She hissed in a breath and studied the toes of her sodden sneakers.

"I need to confess," he said.

Her insides curdled. Here it came, his admission of guilt. A minute ago, she'd kissed a traitor in relief at finding him alive and now almost kissed him again. What a pitiful specimen she was. Maddie stared at the curtain of water streaming past the cave opening.

"When I landed at the bottom of this draw and figured I was a goner," he continued, "my biggest regret was you. I never got the chance to hold you close like I've wanted to do since our days in that Arizona training camp."

"Well, now you've gotten that itch out of your system. You should be happy." Her words came out taut and bitter, not flippant as she'd intended.

Chris's finger on her lips laid a barrier against further sniping remarks.

"I'm anything but happy…and that should make *you* happy," he said. "I can't fall for you, but I don't know how to stop myself, any more than I could halt my tumble into this ravine."

Maddie snorted. "I know why I won't let myself give in to foolish attraction for a handsome face and charming personality. What's your excuse?"

"Ouch! That was harsh."

Heat scalded through her veins. Shame? Why should she be ashamed of insulting a traitor? *But what if he isn't?* The still, small voice sent a tiny shiver through her that had nothing to do with the wet weather. What was that sensation? Hope? The feeling was foreign and familiar all at once—like unexpectedly encountering an old friend she'd lost touch with aeons ago. She didn't dare renew the friendship. Not yet.

Maddie cleared her throat. "Don't take it too badly. At least I called you handsome and charming."

A low chuckle answered her. "I meant your statement was harsh toward yourself."

"Huh?"

"Madeleine Jameson, you are a beauty, inside and out, and don't even know it. You're the whole package—courage, character and intelligence wrapped up in attractive femininity."

"I'm feminine? I mean, attractive? You think so?"

Her heart started performing funky dance moves inside her rib cage. Growing up in an army household hadn't provided fertile soil for producing anybody's version of a homecoming queen. But something inside her had hungered to hear such words. Why did this man have to be the one to speak them?

"No thinking necessary." He shook his head. "And that's why you're a lethal threat to my vow never again to fall for someone during the heat of an investigation. Feelings impair good judgment, and that mistake cost me too much in the past for me to repeat it."

"What happened to sour you on romance on the job?" Her voice cracked, botching her attempt at a casual tone.

Chris released a long breath. "Do you remember when I saw that woman in a wheelchair? For a few seconds I thought I was seeing my sister."

"Your sister?" The air in her lungs went buoyant. So Serena hadn't been an old flame he was tripping out over. She should feel guilty for being so delighted. His poor sister was crippled.

"Back over a decade ago," he continued, "when I was a cub reporter working for a print rag in Los Angeles, I ran across a fresh clue in a cold murder case and became obsessed with exposing the truth."

"Like you are now?"

A deep chuckle answered her. "Touché. But back then I was like a puppy tearing up a pea patch. This was all a game. After interviewing the main suspect from when the murder occurred, I became convinced that she was a victim of unfounded police harassment and forevermore condemned to live under a cloud of baseless suspicion, unless I, Ace Reporter, could figure out who really committed the crime and clear her name. Robin was smart... beautiful...and oh, so charming. Despite the many warnings I'd received from mentors about getting emotionally involved with the subject of an investigation, I fell top over tail for her."

"Only she wasn't innocent?"

"You got that right." Chris snorted. "When my investigation managed to dig up a piece of solid evidence that pointed straight at her, I was devastated. I went over to my sister Serena's house to pour my heart out. Rena and I had always been close, and I needed to unburden myself before turning my evidence over to the police. To abbreviate an ugly story, Robin showed up with a gun, determined to eliminate me and my evidence. Just as Robin pulled the trigger, my sister threw herself in front of me and..." His weighted tones faded away to silence.

Thunder rumbled, but the sound was more distant than a minute ago, and the fury of the rain had diminished. Maddie's heart hung in her chest as heavy as the weather. Chris blamed himself for his sister's injury. Who wouldn't? But the finger-pointing wasn't entirely rational or deserved. "She saved your life...and hers, actually."

"Rena saved her own life by becoming paralyzed from the waist down?" Chris's tone was incredulous.

"This Robin woman would have killed you both on the spot, but I assume your sister's heroic action gave you an opportunity to disarm Robin."

"How did you know?"

"I've seen you operate. You're not ranger trained, but you're no slouch, either."

"Thanks...I think."

"What happened to Robin?"

A deep sigh answered her. "She's serving life without parole, and so is my sister—in a wheelchair. Ever since then, I've made it a maxim of my life never to become emotionally involved with anyone associated with an investigation."

"Sorry for tempting you to compromise your rules of engagement."

She grinned into the dark that had grown less murky while they talked. Why was she so giddy about Chris's all-but-declaration of feelings for her? She didn't want him to care for her romantically, did she? Who was she kidding? Her heart was already seriously compromised. Did that mean she trusted him? Oh, how she wanted to have faith without reservation in his integrity, but her slain comrades in arms wouldn't permit the luxury, not until she had proof positive that he wasn't involved in their deaths.

The rain had practically ceased, but water lapped at the toes of her shoes. Lapped at the toes of her shoes! The breath snagged in her lungs. She was a complete airhead—distracted by all this heart-to-heart blather. Her carelessness could end both of their lives.

"We need to get out of here."

"Sounds good. The rain storm is about over."

"No, I mean we need to get out of this ravine—now!" She splashed him with the water rising over their shoes.

Chris hissed in a breath. "The storm may have passed over this spot, but it's still dumping a ton of water up-ravine."

"And it's all headed downstream straight at us."

"Flash flood!"

Maddie's bones chilled. The words struck terror into the heart of any Texan.

Pulse rampaging through his veins, Chris leaped from the cave, hand in hand with Maddie. Pain in his left ankle sent a whimper to his lips, but he refused to let the sound escape. They had maybe a minute or two—but no longer—and then a rushing wall of water would overtake them, crush them amongst rocks and debris and drown them.

His gaze searched the crevice in the earth that held them trapped. Now that the cloud cover was dissipating, the light of a half-moon painted a ghostly shimmer across sheer and dripping rock-and-clay walls.

"There's no way to climb out?"

Maddie shined the beam of her flashlight on the knotted end of a rope dangling above their heads. "Too high to reach, even for you."

"Wait a second!" He grabbed Maddie's wrist and adjusted the angle of the flashlight beam. "An exposed tree root. You could climb up on that and reach the end of the rope."

"Good idea. You first. Hurry!"

Chris swallowed. "I don't think my leg will support a climb. You go. Go now!"

Maddie stuck her face in his. "Listen up, Mason, if you don't go, I won't, so suck it up and climb."

Stubborn woman! Who did she think she was? A drill sergeant? Didn't she know he needed her to be safe, no matter what happened to him? But he read no compromise in her fierce gaze. For both their sakes he'd better play the obedient grunt this time. Water was already swirling above their calves.

Teeth gritted, Chris grabbed a shiny bend in the protruding root and heaved himself onto it. Pain shot stars in front of his eyes as he dug his toes into the precarious perch and reached upward. The beam of Maddie's light guided his fingers to the end of the rope. On the strength of his arms and the assistance of one good leg to brace himself, he inched his way upward. The rope was slick in his fingers, scraping skin raw, but he dared not slacken his grip.

What was that terrible grinding sound? The growl of the approaching flood?

Chris increased his pace, ankle screaming at him to halt, to let go, to give up. Not going to happen. Maddie depended on him to get out of her path to safety. Fast! Muscles straining…quivering…he hauled himself over the lip of the draw and flopped onto his back.

Thunder bore down on them.

Not thunder!

Roaring water.

Ignoring the throb of fire in his ankle, Chris rolled onto

his stomach and peered over the edge of the draw. Maddie was on her way up, but she'd never make it. The flood was coming. It was here!

Tasting bitter bile on his tongue, Chris reached for her.

EIGHT

The flood waters loomed—a roiling monster bounding toward her, eager for fresh prey. Death's rush planted stillness in Maddie's core. No fear, only peace.

Then a strong hand closed around her wrist, lifted her and dragged her up and over the edge of the ravine even as flood waves pawed at her feet. She rolled across sodden but solid ground. Safe. She lay on her back atop the lumpy remains of her pack, breathing in—out—in—out, staring at stars she never believed she'd see again.

"Are you all right?" Chris's winded voice penetrated her wonderment.

He sprawled beside her, panting and releasing small groans.

Weakness saturated her limbs, but she struggled onto one elbow and gazed into his face. Deep lines on either side of his drawn mouth testified to pain. "I'm fine, but you, my hero, are not."

"Tell me about it." He started a smile that became a grimace.

"Let me take a look at that ankle. I lost the flashlight during my climb, so I'll have to eyeball it as best I can." She sat up and rolled Chris's left pant leg away from the affected area. "Youch! That's not an ankle. It's a basketball."

"Feels like a torch stuck to the end of my leg."

"Most likely a bad sprain. Believe it or not, a sprain can hurt more and swell bigger than a break."

"Whatever it is, I'm not going to get around very fast or very far."

"We have to make it back to the vehicle. I have a first-aid kit in the glove compartment that contains stretch wrap, pain pills and an instant ice pack. Or should we hazard a stop at a hospital E.R.? I could be wrong. That ankle may be broken and should be in a cast."

"Nix on the hospital. We poked our fingers into a red ants' nest last night. The lower profile we keep, the better. I want to live to enjoy my misery."

A chuckle spurted between Maddie's lips, but she quickly sobered. "Let me see if I can find anything around here that will do for a homemade crutch."

The best she could come up with was a notched stick that was too short and acted more like a cane than a crutch. Maddie gladly accepted his arm around her shoulders as they hobbled along. A hazy dawn found them at last approaching Ginger, where the faithful old girl awaited their return behind a stand of trees about a quarter of a mile from where they'd staged their stakeout of the paper factory.

Chris expelled a sharp hiss as Maddie helped him ease into the car. She stepped back and took stock of his pale, dirt-streaked face and bloodshot eyes. If she looked a smidgeon as bedraggled and filthy as he did, she'd make a fine scarecrow.

"Why don't we find some fleabag motel that won't look at us too closely where we can go to ground for a while?"

Chris responded with a thumbs-up, leaned his head back against the rest and closed his eyes. Maddie headed the car down the double-dogleg road that would take them off one of the higher hillsides in the relatively flat topography of this patch of south Texas. Near the first curve, the water of the Rio Grande glinted at her from below. Foot steady on the accelerator, she narrowly skirted the paltry length of guardrail as she navigated the sharp turn.

A hiss from her passenger drew her attention. His eyes were wide open, and he gripped the edges of his seat.

Maddie chuckled. "Yes, I know I drive this thing too fast, but speed and traction are among Ginger's joys."

Chris shook his head and offered a lopsided smile. "Sorry. I'm a little punchy right now. After ducking bullets and escaping a flood, I'd just as soon not land nose-down on the riverbank."

"Gotcha, sarge." She saluted him.

He snorted and subsided against his seat.

She drove them to a run-down section of the city and checked them into a pair of adjoining motel rooms. No credit card. Cash only. That was the way she traveled now. Then she helped Chris into his room. He flopped onto the bed, and she put a pillow underneath his ankle. She went back out to the car and returned with her emergency kit and his piece of small carry-on luggage that he'd stowed in Ginger's backseat when he first broke into her vehicle at the parking garage in San Antonio.

"Here. Pop a couple of these."

Chris obediently downed the pain pills, then went still, eyes shut, but he was awake. Pain furrows between his eyebrows gave him away.

"I'm going to take a quick shower and run to the store after more ice packs. One's not going to be enough. And I'll round up something for us to eat. Then I'll be back to wrap your ankle."

"You're amazing," he murmured.

Forty-five minutes later, she knocked on his door, then

leaned on the frame to await Chris's hobble across the floor to let her in—if he was even awake. At least she felt halfway human and presentable now. A night without sleep wasn't that unusual for an army ranger, but probably unheard-of for a civilian journalist.

"Who is it?" His voice came from the other side of the door.

Good boy. He wasn't assuming the identity of his caller. "It's me. Maddie."

The chain rattled and the dead bolt clicked open. Another kudo. He'd gotten up after her departure and secured the entrance. The door swung wide, and so did Maddie's mouth. Not only had he locked himself in, but he'd taken a shower and changed his clothes. Those pain pills must be phenomenal. Then she looked at his face. It was ashen, and the puckers between his brows hadn't lost any depth.

"You'd better sit down before you fall down," she said.

He grunted and hopped to the only chair in the room— an overstuffed beast upholstered with faded brown cloth. Maddie pulled up the matching ottoman and held his ankle between her knees while she applied cold packs and bound it in stretch wrap. He never flinched or made a sound during the process, but his knuckles went white from his grip on the chair arms.

"There. I'm done torturing you."

"What time is it?"

"Coming up on 8:00 a.m."

"Click on the TV, would you? We should be able to catch the morning news on one of the stations. The internet news through my phone isn't showing any updates that mention our names, but I'd still like to verify that on live TV."

Maddie huffed. "Well, at least our exploits at the paper factory haven't made the news."

"I don't think those jokers want anyone to know about the midnight meeting we crashed."

"I wish we could figure out who Agent Ramsey was talking to in that office."

"Did you catch a glimpse of any of those others while we were playing cat and mouse in the plant?"

"Negative."

"Me, either."

"Bummer." Maddie sighed and clicked the power button on the remote.

Canned laughter invaded the room from some inane sitcom, and she quickly flipped the channels until she found talking news heads. She picked up one of the carry-out bags she'd brought from a nearby fast-food joint.

"You hungry?"

"A part of me is ravenous. Another part wonders if I might ralph if I tried to eat."

Maddie wrinkled her nose. "Probably the pain pills doing a number on your empty tummy."

"What have you got?"

Mouth watering, she handed him a wrapped breakfast sandwich and container of juice, then dug her own out of the bag. The smells of sausage and biscuit had nearly driven her nuts on the drive back to the hotel. What was that old Western saying? She was so hungry her stomach thought her throat had been cut. *Ewww!* Bad thought. She took a big chomp out of her sandwich. By the time she'd wolfed down her breakfast, nothing significant to their situation had been said on the news, and Chris had eaten his portion without any ill effects.

Maddie stood, yawning and stretching. "I'm going to catch a few *z*'s. You'd better do the same. See you at twelve hundred hours for another dose of pain medicine and a change of ice packs."

Chris groaned. "Fine, but if I'm sleeping soundly at noon and don't answer after the first knock, go away."

"Deal." Maddie laughed.

She traipsed back to her room, lugging exhaustion like a hundred-pound pack. Who cared that the mattress was lumpy and the linens yellowed? As soon as she fell onto the bed, sleep wrapped her in warm arms. Minutes later, the bedside phone shrilled. Or at least she thought it had only been minutes. A quick check of the clock on the nightstand said noon was only a tick away.

Maddie sat up and grabbed the insistent handset. "Hello?" Her voice came out thick.

"Get over here. Fast!" Chris's voice barked. "The ad for the upcoming newscast is promising a special segment on developments in the Jackson murder case, and they're tying it to the Rio Grande Massacre. Some bigwig on the Texas Homeland Security and Public Safety Committee is going to address the public live. Seems he's known for his vendetta against the drug trade and has taken a personal interest in the case."

Sleep's dregs sloughed off Maddie, and she leaped from her semi-comfortable nest. Within a few seconds, she joined Chris in staring at the television screen in his room. He occupied his easy chair, and Maddie took up a perch on the end of the bed, hands gripping her knees. A sober-faced anchorman gazed back at them as he made his announcements.

"Breaking news in the recent murder of Agent Edgar Jackson of the federal Drug Enforcement Agency. The police now have suspects who were witnessed fleeing the scene. Their identities link the crime to last year's massacre of a joint task force charged with rounding up the Ortiz Drug Cartel near Nuevo Laredo, Mexico."

A pair of faces appeared side by side, filling the screen.

Maddie's stomach plummeted to her toes. She gaped at her stern-eyed, military image—hair scraped back into a severe bun—next to Chris's engaging smile. Viewers might not have too much trouble imagining her as a murderer, but Chris? He looked like the wholesome boy next door.

"Madeleine Jerrard, former communications expert for the army ranger team wiped out in the Rio Grande Massacre and television news reporter Christopher Mason, formerly associated with that same unit, are sought in connection with the death of Agent Jackson. Anyone spotting these suspects is to report their location to the police at once, but do not approach them. Repeat, do not approach them. They are considered armed and dangerous."

A poke in the ribs turned Maddie's attention toward her companion.

"Do you think the guy at the front desk when you checked in will remember us?"

"There's always a chance, but not a good one. He never saw you and barely glanced at me. Absorbed in some girlie magazine he was drooling over."

Chris nodded, and his gaze strayed from her toward the television screen. Their attention refocused on the news report.

The anchorman drew himself up straighter and squared his shoulders. "Now we take you, live, to Laredo police headquarters for a statement from State Representative Donald Jess, a Laredo native and Chairman of the Texas Homeland Security and Public Safety Committee."

The scene morphed to an outside view of the glass-fronted entrance of the Laredo police headquarters. A crowd had gathered to hear a short, pudgy man, who stood on the sidewalk behind a portable podium. Flanking the man and behind him stood various officials. A few wore guns at their hips and badges on their chests, but most betrayed their law enforcement status in their bearing and the look in their eyes. Some DEA agents among them, certainly, though not Agent Clyde Ramsey. A couple of individuals in suits and ties were also packing sidearms, judging by the telltale bulges beneath their jackets.

She leaned in closer to the picture. "FBI, for sure," she said out loud to Chris.

"Who?"

"Second suit to the left. I remember him from the investigation following the Rio Grande Massacre. The Federal Bureau of Investigation was not involved in the mission against the Ortiz Cartel, but after the op blew up, they were tasked with the job of figuring out what went wrong. This guy—" she pointed to the TV screen "—introduced himself as Special Agent Blunt. Heavy on the *special*. He interviewed me while I was still in the hospital. A real jerk. Walks like his shoes are too small. I don't know the agent next to him."

"Shh! The representative is talking."

Maddie huffed and swallowed the rest of her comments.

"...country lost a valuable asset to its national security when Agent Edgar Jackson was gunned down in cold blood," said the man behind the podium.

Maddie's mouth went dry, and beside her, Chris's hiss of indrawn breath betrayed that he'd heard the same thing she did—the voice of the calm man from the midnight meeting at the paper plant. No wonder the guy's voice seemed familiar last night. She'd heard Jess on TV from time to time, spouting off about "the war on drugs." Her head spun. A state representative charged with oversight of public safety and security, such as border patrols, was in the pocket of the drug cartel? How perfect for them.

"We do not yet know for sure why Agent Jackson was gunned down two nights ago," Jess continued, "but we have suspects that we believe can answer that question when they are apprehended."

The representative slid his hands forward so that his thick fingers gripped the front edges of the podium. The motion suggested a man struggling to contain great emotion.

Maddie's lip curled. Jess had missed his calling to the Big Screen. He modeled outraged innocence while setting up the truly innocent to take the fall for his crimes. Brilliant, but twisted beyond what she could fathom. Is this frame-up what the other mystery man had meant when he said "the problem" with the "nosy reporter" was being addressed? After last night, Jess and his accomplices would know Chris and she were together and target them with a manhunt.

Maddie shook herself. In her rapid-fire speculations, she'd missed some of what Jess was saying.

"…Jackson was unsatisfied by the findings of the task force assigned to investigate the Rio Grande Massacre and was pursuing inquiries on his own time. Perhaps that is the answer to why he is now dead. Perhaps he had discovered that Madeleine Jerrard and Christopher Mason were not lucky survivors of the massacre, but accomplices of the Ortiz Drug Cartel. Reason enough for the desperate pair to take Agent Jackson's life. Jerrard and Mason were seen at the murdered agent's home the night of his death."

Yeah, right! By whom? Sure, there was an off chance some neighbor had parted their curtains and seen two figures fleeing the scene, but there was no way she and Chris were identifiable in the dark. This was another pure fabrication—a wily frame-up and one that would incite the entire public against them.

The state representative's cheeks puffed in and out as his gaze swept his audience. "If these two are innocent, they should not mind giving themselves up and submitting to proper questioning. But if they do not voluntarily turn themselves in, I call upon the citizens of my home city to aide law enforcement in bringing them to justice by keeping a lookout and reporting their whereabouts to the authorities immediately. You may do so by calling 9-1-1, your local police department, or utilizing the number that will be posted on your television screen. This will connect you directly to the FBI field office in San Antonio."

Maddie's stomach turned inside out. How did she and Chris prove this man's complicity with drug runners? All the authority lay in the state representative's hands, and now they were made out to be killers...and worse. Her fingernails gnawed at her palms.

A movement directly behind the speaker caught her eye, and a new face edged into view—three quarters of the face anyway. The heat in Maddie's veins went arctic in a nanosecond.

A memory bullied its way into her consciousness. She'd seen this man before. In the desert. Under a full moon. The shadow of a creosote bush blocked out exactly as much of his face as was now covered by Representative Jess. The memory was associated with lying on the pebbled ground, ears ringing, pain throbbing in her leg, her head. She'd opened her eyes, and there he loomed. Then a familiar click—the cock of a gun—and a moon glint on the barrel of a weapon aimed in her direction. After that, memory blanked out once more.

What was this man doing at the site of the Rio Grande Massacre? Did he show up during the attack or after? Where was she when she saw him? In camp? Somewhere out in the desert where Chris said he carried her? Maybe Chris knew who he was. Maybe they had a rendezvous out there in the wilderness. Why did the guy intend to shoot her, and what—or who—stopped him? The answers were shrouded in dark dread.

Limbs quivering, scarcely able to draw a full breath, Maddie rose and pointed at the television screen. "Who is that man?"

Chris squinted toward the set and made out a partial face and sections of a pair of broad shoulders. "I have no idea. Never saw him before."

"You're sure?" Maddie's stare sifted through him.

His gut clenched. What did she suspect him of now? "I. Do. Not. Know. Him. And I have an excellent memory for faces and names. Comes with the job territory."

Maddie's jaw worked like she had more to say but hadn't decided what it should be. The rigid set of her shoulders eased marginally, and she returned her attention to the television, where Jess was wrapping up his address. "I saw him. Out there. In the desert."

Chris let out a low whistle. "Watch!" He pointed toward fresh activity on the screen.

The camera followed Representative Jess as he strode in the direction of a dark Town Car waiting at the curb. The mystery man traveled in his wake. Now that Chris could see more of the guy, the exposed shoulder holster strapped over his short-sleeved polo shirt marked him as—what? Not law enforcement. Bodyguard? The guy made a formidable barrier to mayhem on the state representative, with or without the gun. His upper arm muscles rivaled Popeye's.

Maddie rose as the news program returned to the television studio, and the weatherman commenced predicting more dry heat. Chris's gaze followed her as she prowled from one end of the small room to the other. Her fixed stare focused on nothing in the room, including him. She was wrapped in her own thoughts, perhaps struggling to grasp more memories. Maybe he could help her—help them both—by connecting a few dots about Jess and his pet pit bull. An internet search could reveal a lot.

He picked up his phone from the lamp table beside him. "A little research on Jess is in order. I'd like to unearth his connection to that printing factory, as well as the identity of his muscle-bound shadow. I suspect he's a bodyguard, but that begs the question why Jess thinks he needs one. Few government officials employ one on their own dime, and even fewer rate government-paid protection on a routine basis."

"Did you stop him from shooting me?"

The demand from Maddie halted Chris in the act of pressing his thumb to his cell phone screen. "Who was going to shoot you?"

"The mystery guy with Jess." Her statement bristled like he was slow in the head.

"That man held a gun on you?"

Maddie expelled a sharp breath in his direction. "A gun *is* the most common tool used to shoot someone. Where *were* you?"

"I have no idea. I—"

She stomped up to him and loomed over him. "I remember enough to think I wasn't in camp during this incident. You said you moved me into the desert. You must have been there."

"Not necessarily. I told you I left you to go get help. Remember?"

"So this guy shows up out of the blue exactly where I'm lying? You need a better story than that."

Chris's throat tightened. It must be maddening to want to remember something, but only finding bits and pieces. How did he get her to trust him through the blank spots?

"Maybe he followed the sound and flash of your handgun."

"The flash of my—" Maddie's jaw flopped open and remained that way as if she was speechless. Then she shut her mouth with an audible click of teeth and planted her hands on her hips. "The investigator's report said my handgun was missing from its holster when I was found. They never recovered the weapon. Did you take it and use it? Why were you shooting? At what or whom?"

Enough was enough of being raked over the coals for something he hadn't done. Chris lowered his foot from the ottoman. His ankle issued loud protests, and sweat sprang to his forehead, but he rose to his full height and gazed down at the bottled fury before him.

"You can choose to believe me or not. I never touched your gun. You fired it. If you'll listen for a minute, I'll explain what happened."

"Stop!" She pointed to the phone in his hand. "When did you last use that?"

The urgency in her tone stalled the rush of words on Chris's lips. He'd longed for this opportunity to tell her the whole story. Get everything out in the open. But some fresh crisis had painted horror on her face.

"All right. You caught me. When I woke up about a minute or two before I called you on the room phone, I called my station and let my producer know I was among the living and still on the story. But don't worry—I didn't tell her where I was."

Maddie's lips thinned into a slash, and her gaze nailed him to the wall. "But you did tell the FBI."

"What?"

"In case the fact escaped you, there's now a manhunt on for us armed-and-dangerous criminals. The feds will have pulled your cell number and put a trace on it."

"But I only spoke for a minute or two with my boss."

Maddie rolled her eyes. "Get with the times, Mason. I'm a communications expert, remember? Digital traces are practically instant. Every available law enforcement officer in the vicinity could be surrounding us as we speak. We have to go. Now!"

Chris gaped at his cell. Maddie snatched it from his hand and hurled it across the room. The phone struck the bathroom door frame and shattered into pieces. The sound electrified Chris into action. He grabbed his billfold from the side table and stuffed it into a back pocket of his slacks and then reached for the handle of his carry on case.

"Leave it!" Maddie barked. "Leave everything. We may already be too late."

A distant sound plucked at Chris's awareness. He hissed in a breath. Sirens!

NINE

Maddie helped Chris hobble to the car. A drop of sweat plopped from his chin onto her shoulder. Sure, it was hot out here. The power of the sun had already licked up every drop from this morning's puddles on the tarmac. But Chris's perspiration probably owed more to pain than summer weather.

She eased Chris into Ginger's front passenger seat and raced to the driver's side, gaze darting around the area. Sirens blared closer…closer, but the few pedestrians treading the sidewalks seemed indifferent. This was the sort of neighborhood that would find such sounds commonplace.

Shaking her head, she revved Ginger's engine and threw her into Reverse. She was an idiot for leaving a journalist alone with a smart phone. Of course, she hadn't known when she turned in for a nap that an official manhunt had been organized for the two of them. Only a few hours ago, that consequence was a possibility but not a reality. Now they were in the pressure cooker for real.

Maddie peeled out of the parking lot onto the street, shooting past a city bus. The bus driver laid on his horn. She spared no glance over her shoulder. No point in holding Ginger back now. They needed to be out of view before the approaching units reached the motel. If that was possible. She squealed around a corner on two tires. Chris let out an audible groan.

"They wanted us to run." Chris's words sounded like they oozed out from between gritted teeth.

"Why do you say that?" She glanced at his drawn profile. He didn't meet her gaze.

"Why announce their approach when it would work so much easier to surround us first and then command our surrender? Chances are better that way of taking us peacefully and without harm to ourselves or others—since they're under the impression we're trigger-happy."

Maddie concentrated on driving. A yellow light loomed ahead. She had to beat its change to red. Ginger's nose reached the opposite side of the intersection as the light went crimson. Boarded up businesses, porn shops and bars flashed past on either side of them.

"I see what you mean," she said. "Our enemies know we didn't kill Jackson, but they set us up so that when we run we look guilty and give the cops a reason to take us down—with deadly force, if necessary."

"Your mama didn't raise no dummy."

"Yours, either. So someone high on the food chain needed to order the foot soldiers to charge with sirens blaring."

She guided Ginger into another turn on a dime. Good. A residential area lay ahead. Cruising quiet streets and avenues stood a better chance of avoiding detection than making a beeline toward a well-traveled highway, even though they could move faster. Maddie slowed the Oldsmobile to the top end of the speed limit.

"Jess qualifies under the definition of *high up*," Chris said, "but it's unlikely he'd have direct say over law enforcement personnel."

"So someone with clout in the Laredo police department must be a coconspirator?"

"Or someone in the FBI or DEA. Once the feds get their teeth into a case, the local PD tends to take a backseat. Anything to do with the Rio Grande Massacre would have high priority on a federal level."

Maddie's gaze rifled through the neighborhood…cataloguing…searching. There! She turned the car up a private driveway to a run-down home and brought Ginger to a halt beneath a vacant car port. Sirens wailed blocks away, but they were stationary now. No doubt filling that motel parking lot with flashing lights and badges.

"Why are we stopping?" Chris asked.

She pointed upward as a throaty *whump-whump* from overhead announced the approach of a chopper. "Air surveillance. I expected it to show up pretty quickly."

"But we can't stay here," he said. "We didn't exactly slip away from that motel unnoticed. They'll have a description of our vehicle in short order and start a systematic ground search of the area. Plus they'll broadcast a BOLO. Then every member of every law enforcement agency for hundreds of miles, not to mention everyone with a police band scanner, will be on the lookout for a classic Oldsmobile Cutlass."

Maddie barked a laugh. "I know one bus driver who will gladly give the cops a description of Ginger." She sobered as a lump invaded her throat. "We're going to have to ditch her."

Her hands fisted around the steering wheel. Why was everything she loved wrenched away from her? It was too painful to invest her heart in anything. In her world, caring got you hurt, and trusting got you dead. Maddie inhaled a deep breath and let it out slowly.

Stop feeling sorry for yourself, Jerrard. Suck it up.

You're a ranger...or you were a ranger. Make your unit proud. Do the right thing, or lay down your life trying.

"As soon as that air surveillance moves off, we'll make a break for it," she said.

"That's the best plan you have?"

Maddie met Chris's steady stare. "Unless you have a better one. This isn't the planning phase of an operation. It's execution time, and a hundred times out of a hundred, the best-planned op takes an unexpected twist that requires grunts to think on their feet. That's how training complements planning. And in this case, we've been winging it since we found Agent Jackson's dead body."

Chris's hand folded over hers on the steering wheel. The warmth feathered comfort to her heart. If only she could lean into his strong arms like she'd allowed herself to do when they were trapped in that gorge in the middle of a rain-lashed night. Now she had to stay tough—focused. She pulled away. On a sigh, Chris returned his hand to his lap, though his gaze never left her.

"Injured, I'm a liability to you," he said. "How about letting me take Ginger and lead the cops on a wild-goose chase. They'll catch me eventually, but that will give you a chance to get away. Now that we've identified Jess as a major snake in the traitors' nest, I have no doubt you'll find a way to expose the infestation and see that justice is served."

Except for the absurdity of his words, the unexpected tenderness in Chris's eyes would have unleashed the tears contained in that lump in her throat. "You're certifiable, Mason." Her voice came out scratchy. "Your investigative methods got us this far, and without your access to the world's ear, all I can do is run. I've proved that so far. If anyone is expendable, it's me."

Chris grimaced. "Looks like we're stuck with each other."

"Looks like. I don't hear that chopper anymore. They've moved off to scout in a different direction. I'm going to try to get us to the nearest bus station, where we can ditch Ginger."

"And hop a bus to Timbuktu?"

"Good grief, no. That's what we want them to think—that we've fled the city. While they're chasing down buses in every direction, we'll hole up in another dive where you can rest your leg, and we can indulge in a little of that planning you crave."

Chris flashed his captivating megawatt smile, and Maddie's heart *ka-bumped* against her ribs. She ordered it to be quiet and settle down. If ever there would be time for romance in her life, she hadn't found it yet. His explanation about what happened after he carted her away from the besieged camp was incomplete and unconvincing. They needed to identify the mystery man who'd held a gun on her that night on the Rio Grande, and the guy had better have no connection to Chris. If she couldn't put to rest her last niggling doubt about Chris, the time for love might be never.

"We've got company on our seven." Chris's gut twisted into a Gordian knot.

They were twenty minutes into Maddie's circuitous route toward the Greyhound bus station near the river, and they'd just chanced hopping onto a freeway to make time. One second they were cruising along in cop-free traffic, and Chris had started to believe they might make their goal without incident. The next moment, he glanced over his shoulder and caught the sun's rays glinting off a set of bubble lights atop a sedan creeping up on them in the left lane.

"Roger that," Maddie said. "Do you think they see us?"

"Not yet, but that could change as soon as they get closer."

"I'm taking the next exit. Either we'll get lucky, or we'll land in a car chase that stands a strong chance of ending badly for us. You ready?"

Chris tightened his seat belt. "I don't know that we have a choice. It's ready-or-not time."

The *tick-tock* of the turn signal echoed through his head like a countdown toward disaster. Maddie eased the car onto the exit ramp as if gliding on butter. She was a stellar driver. If anyone could make this unusual vehicle all but invisible, she could. They turned onto a busy side street with no sign of the police cruiser on their bumper.

"We made it!" Chris sucked in a full breath then spurted a laugh.

"Don't count your chickadees yet, buckaroo. I need to see no police activity on our tails for the next five minutes before I'll breathe easy."

"Negative Nelly." Chris offered a lopsided grin.

"Cautious Cassandra would be more accurate, Bubble Boy." She answered his grin.

Chris chuckled. "Let's hope my bubble doesn't get busted then."

"I can agree with that. Change of plan. It's taking too long to reach the main Greyhound terminal. By now, the place is probably crawling with cops, since any type of public transit would be seen as a potential destination for us. Fliers with our mugs plastered on them might already be posted all over the airport, taxi stands and car rental places, too. Not that anyone would need to see a flier to recognize your famous face."

Chris snorted. "Fame is one thing. Infamy is another. Who knows? Maybe we've made the FBI's Ten Most Wanted list."

"If we don't find a way to clear our names soon, we will."

"What's the new plan?"

"Remember that down-at-the-heels truck stop on the edge of the city where a few of us stopped last year to recon for the upcoming mission?"

"I remember their outstanding biscuits and gravy."

Maddie chuckled. "Just like a man. Connecting memory to his stomach."

"A harmless and effective masculine quirk." Chris grinned. "Are we going to hitch a ride on an eighteen-wheeler or just leave Ginger to be found so they'll think we did?"

"We'll do whatever seems best at the time. But if we hitch a ride, we don't want the driver to know he has passengers."

"That's what I like about this being on the run—loads of spontaneity."

"Think of it as ad libbing. Might make more sense to you that way."

Fifteen minutes later, they reached the outskirts of the city, and the sprawling gas station, truck wash, fix-it garage, and greasy spoon restaurant with the great biscuits and gravy came into view. The interconnected, metal-sided buildings perched on a stretch of dusty plain flanked by desert on the far side and the Rio Grande River behind.

"This isn't far from the paper factory."

"No, it isn't."

Maddie's response was terse, discouraging further conversation. She wore her high-alert expression, gaze devouring the layout. If so much as a gecko escaped her notice, he'd be stunned.

Chris's mouth watered involuntarily as she turned the nose of the Oldsmobile into the massive parking lot. Fat chance they'd wander inside for a meal, though his morning biscuit had long dissolved from his insides. Hunger was the least of their problems.

The tarmac was occupied by long rows of semis, a few with their diesel engines chugging. If they wanted to vamoose, they shouldn't have a big problem finding transportation that would pull out soon and take them to who knew where. Destination might not matter at the moment.

"I'm going to park on the far side of the restaurant," Maddie said. "It's a better place to abandon a car than out front."

"Go for it."

They left the cover of the semis and pulled around the corner of the restaurant. Maddie's sudden mash on the brakes threw Chris against his seat belt. He gaped at the sight before him. If he'd tried to imagine the worst disaster they could encounter, he wouldn't have come close to this one.

Half a dozen assorted law enforcement vehicles poked their bumpers toward the side of the restaurant—a couple of Smokies, two sheriff's vehicles, a Texas Ranger pickup and a city police cruiser. Had they happened on a cop convention, or was this a hot spot for coffee and donuts? Maybe the local law enforcement community agreed with him about the biscuits and gravy. Whatever the attraction, a state patrolman stood by the door of his vehicle, staring straight at them. Then he ripped his radio from his belt.

Maddie threw the Oldsmobile into Reverse, spitting loose rocks up under the chassis. The hairs on the nape of Chris's neck stood up. The *pop-pop-pop* was too close to the sound of gunfire to suit him—not when they might be the targets of real bullets very soon. Maddie cranked the wheel, and Ginger performed a skidding about face, then rocketed out of the parking lot. Sirens were already starting to wail in their wake.

"We've been through plans A, B and C." Chris gripped the edge of the armrest. "Have we got a plan D?"

"This is more like plan Z," she said, gaze straight ahead, jaw and cheekbones jutting.

"This is nuts! You're heading toward the paper plant?" Chris ground out. "What are we going to do—ram through the front glass doors and demand to know where the drugs are?"

Maddie's lack of response stabbed a shaft of ice through his middle. What was this woman planning? She'd better let him in on it.

"If you'd—"

"Wait!" She showed him the palm of her hand.

Chris ground his teeth together.

She threw the Oldsmobile into another gear and revved the vehicle up the grade that led to the ridge where they'd staked out the plant. He looked over his shoulder. The law enforcement vehicles had lost a little ground, but they weren't far enough behind to ditch them. And sure not on this narrow road that offered no side streets for miles. Trees and brush crowded them on either side.

Maddie whipped the Cutlass around a dogleg turn, slowed and stopped in the middle of the road. The cop vehicles were out of sight, but not out of sound. They were gaining by the second.

She gazed at him, calm purpose in her eyes. "Get out."

"No."

Her hand wound around his, and the steel in her gaze softened. She leaned close and pressed tender lips against his. "Do you want to know the truth, Mason? I'm losing the battle against my attraction for you."

Her touch, her words bumped his heart rate up another notch, if that were possible. He reached for her, but she pulled away—not far, but far enough.

"Trust me."

He nodded, the ability to speak crushed beneath a boulder weighting his chest.

"Get out and take cover in the brush beside the road. Don't move. Don't make a sound. No matter what you hear. Do it *now,* or we're both goners."

As if he'd somehow detached from himself and was watching someone else go through the motions, Chris opened the car door. Pain sizzled up his body as he levered himself out onto the pavement, but the sensation seemed light-years distant and of no consequence. If it would take them to safety, he'd carry Maddie in his arms a hundred miles on his bum leg. Not that she'd let him try.

Midafternoon heat roared up from the tarmac and thrust him into an instant sauna, but a chill shook him from the inside out as he limped into the brush. What was Maddie planning? Something she didn't dare tell him.

Ginger's engine roared. Chris glanced over his shoulder, and the car was speeding away. Sirens were closing in. He ducked down and lay flat against an incline behind a huddle of bushes. Cop cars whizzed past him in quick succession, throwing waves of dry heat onto his back with their passage. Ginger had already disappeared around a turn, but there was no chance Maddie could escape. Her pursuers would have radioed ahead. She'd meet roadblocks sooner rather than later.

Was she doing the reverse of what he'd suggested earlier—letting herself be caught so he could escape? Not such a great plan, considering his injury. How would he even manage to hobble back to the truck stop, much less stow himself away in a semi? And where would he go? Maddie was the clandestine operative, not him.

Did she actually admit she was developing feelings for him? Despite his stoutest resolve, he could say the same where his own heart was concerned. Where did that leave them if they never got the chance to explore the possibilities? He slammed a fist against the side of his knee and paid with a snarl of pain from his ankle.

A horrendous screech of twisted metal and shattering glass pierced the sirens' wails. The sound echoed up from the gorge beyond and below him. Chris's whole being turned to brittle frost.

"Nooooo! God, please!"

The words rasped from his throat as a vision flashed before his mind's eye as clear as anything he'd ever witnessed with his outward senses—Ginger airborne over the low cliff that fronted the Rio Grande. Had Maddie pushed the car beyond its limits, missed a turn and plunged through the flimsy barrier onto the bank below?

Shuddering, Chris buried his face in hot, acrid soil and cried out to God.

TEN

"Are you praying or talking to yourself?" Maddie settled onto the sun-baked ground next to Chris.

His head jerked up, and he devoured her with his gaze. "You!"

She blinked at him. "Yes. Last time I checked I was me."

"You're alive." A medieval knight waking up in the twenty-first century couldn't have spoken with greater amazement.

"I am." She grinned fit to split her face.

Chris scowled blacker than last night's storm. His arm snaked out quick as thought and snatched her to him. Her face was mashed up against a pleasantly broad and sturdy shoulder and his masculine scents of soap and sweat filled her nostrils. She wriggled against him, but he crushed her all the tighter.

"Don't ever scare me like that again." His stern words blew hot in her ear.

Maddie managed to nod against his chest, and his grip loosened. She lifted her head and gazed into his eyes. Had the subtle crow's-feet at their corners deepened since last she saw him? She was lucky his hair hadn't gone white from trauma like his sister's had done.

"I'm sorry," she said. "There wasn't time to explain my plan or argue with you about the risks."

He grunted darkly. "Maybe you could take a moment now and enlighten me? I thought you'd gone over the cliff into the river."

Maddie's heart twisted, and she lowered her gaze. "I bailed at the last second. Now the cops are busy recovering the wreck of the car they think we both occupied, and we have a small window of time to slip away."

"You ditched Ginger? Your brother's car? You *really* ditched her."

Maddie nodded, her throat too full of loss for further speech. A strong finger lifted her chin, and the blue of Chris's eyes pulled her deep into their welcoming embrace. He bent his head, and his mouth touched one corner of hers then the other.

"Madeleine Jerrard," he murmured. "You are the bravest woman I know… Check that. You're the bravest *person* I've ever met."

Something huddled and lonely in Maddie's depths unfurled before the simple power of his affirmation. It would be so easy to surrender to the feelings for him that grew like Virginia creepers and clung to her heart in spite of her best efforts to exterminate them. She had to remember there was no future in love unless trust could also be declared. Her brother always told her she was stubborn beyond belief. Maybe he was right. So far, Chris had seemed to play square with her, but someone from within camp the night of the attack had to have transmitted their location to the cartel. It still made sense that the only other survivor of the carnage was that person.

Please, Dear Lord, could there turn out to be some other explanation?

"Let's get out of here," she said, "before the authorities

figure out that we weren't inside Ginger when she lost her reckless bid to defy gravity."

She helped Chris struggle to his feet.

"Your arms are all scraped and scratched," he said.

She shrugged. "One of the consequences of performing a rolling dive from a fast-moving vehicle."

"Are you hurt elsewhere?"

His concern feathered warmth through her chest. "Nothing serious, but let's just say that most of me will soon turn not-so-pretty colors."

Shaking his head, Chris muttered something she didn't totally catch about daredevil stunts giving him a heart attack. Suppressing a smile, Maddie gathered his arm around her shoulder, and they moved off down a deer track through brush and mesquite. At every step, the hiss of his breath between his teeth tore at her heart. They needed transportation, and he should have professional medical care. *Yeah, right.* Like they could stroll into any urgent care center and walk away without metal bracelets snapped onto their wrists.

"Leave me," Chris said twenty minutes into their trek. "I'm done."

Maddie didn't argue. He'd lost enough moisture from heat and pain to dehydrate him. She let him ease down onto a rock in a narrow cut near the base of the hillside. He slumped, gripping his knees with his hands, and his breath rasped in his chest. From below, the whoosh of occasional traffic from a narrow county road reached their ears, but their location was out of sight of travelers.

"Sorry...I'm such a...drag on you," Chris puffed. "Go on...without me." His blue gaze lifted to hers, and he straightened his shoulders.

"And leave you stranded in the middle of nowhere? Not a chance, Mason."

He waved a dismissive hand. "Do me a favor…call in my location to the feds. They'll collect me fast enough. At least…I'll have food, water and medical care while you hitch that ride to Timbuktu. I mean it. Leave the country if you must in order to be safe and go on with your life."

Maddie pressed the back of her hand to Chris's forehead.

He pulled away, scowling. "What?"

"Just checking to see if you might be delirious from fever." She planted her hands on her hips. "We're a team until this is over, one way or another." Lips pressed tight together, Maddie performed mental calculations. "If I've got my bearings correctly, there's a convenience store about a mile east of here. Settle in under some shade, and I'll be back within the hour with the first two items on your wish list—food and water. I'll even wrangle some form of transportation if I can."

Chris snorted. "And while you're doing that, I'll noodle up an idea that will expose the bad guys and make us heroes instead of heels."

"You do that." She wagged a finger in his face and offered him a jaunty grin—better than allowing him to see the despair that kneaded her gut.

For at least a half hour after Maddie left him, Chris fussed and stewed over their situation and how his injury hampered their mobility. Slumped in the shade of a boulder, he picked up small rocks and chucked them at nearby swatches of mesquite. He might feel better if the brush was some portion of Jess's anatomy or his mystery bodyguard. That pair and everyone connected with their drug-running scheme needed to be taken out of business permanently.

Gradually, his mind turned to the snatches of conversation they'd overheard during the conspirator's clandestine meeting at the paper plant. What had Jess meant about a golden opportunity and the fourth? Fourth what? Was it a number? Or maybe a date. The Fourth of July! The holiday would be upon them in two weeks. Is that when they planned to move a drug shipment across the border? Come to think of it, that foghorn bodyguard's remark about the cops being distracted and run ragged dovetailed perfectly with a Fourth of July smuggling operation. Holidays stressed the manpower of law enforcement agencies in dealing with out-of-hand celebrations, extra traffic and the usual assortment of accidents that occurred when people gathered in masses or handled dangerous items like fireworks.

The few words Maddie and he had overheard that night told a fairly complete story. Who was smuggling the drugs into the country: Fernando Ortiz's cartel operatives and their accomplices on this side of the border. When the drugs were coming in: midnight on the Fourth of July. As well as where they were being received: the Rio Grande Paper Plant with its built-in distribution center.

Chris sighed. If only his recorder hadn't taken a bullet. Without the recording, Maddie and he had no proof to give to the authorities, even if they knew who they dared approach without setting themselves up for assassination.

The distant bay of a dog arrested his thoughts. Breath snagged in his throat. Of course! The cops had figured out that the smashed vehicle that went over the cliff was empty, and now they'd brought in a hound to track the fugitives. With his bum leg, Maddie hadn't been able to drag him far. At the most, he had minutes until he was apprehended. Maybe that was for the best.

Chris struggled to his feet and took a few limping steps, teeth gritted. Sure, his head might tell him to sit quietly and let himself be taken, but something in his core couldn't give up that tamely. A deep anger drove him another few steps on the down-angled path. He couldn't let Jess and his ilk win so easily.

Crack!

Chris froze, staring around. Was someone shooting at him?

No, the sharp blast had come from the roadway not far below, but which remained concealed behind a tumble of rock and brittle chola. He sniffed the air and wrinkled his nose. What a bitter stench! A trickle of black smoke dissipated into the air from the same vicinity as the noise.

The throaty bay of a dog closing in behind him raised the hairs at the base of Chris's neck. He struggled forward. A female figure popped around the crumbling rock slide at the far edge of the road. She was dressed in a dingy white peasant blouse and brightly colored, calf-length skirt that was bound to her slender waist with what looked like twine. Her head was covered by a bandanna scarf. Only the face was the least bit familiar.

"Maddie?"

Instead of answering, she assumed her usual supportive stance with his arm around her shoulder. The feel of her was soft and feminine, but oh, so strong. Would they ever find a time when he could hold her close—offer her comfort and support—instead of being a weight she must bear? Who was he kidding that his heart wasn't already nine-tenths gone in spite of his vow that business and romance must never again mix? People made unkeepable promises to themselves all the time.

"Hustle up, Mason," she hissed. "We've got about ten seconds before that dog nips chunks out of us."

Chris clamped his jaw together and double-timed his limp. Just now, he'd maybe rather shake her than hug her, but she was one hundred percent right.

They made their way around the rock pile, and Chris nearly stumbled when he caught sight of the conveyance filling the narrow gravel shoulder of the road. The Beverly Hillbillies would be right at home in this rattletrap pickup truck with a skewed rear bumper that looked like it was attached to the chassis with the same kind of twine that held Maddie's skirt to her middle. Scarred wooden slats encased the truck bed, and red rust splotched once-blue paint so that the exterior of the truck was the color of a Smurf with the measles. The acrid trail of black exhaust spewed by the chugging engine explained the backfire noise and smoke stink from seconds before.

"Get in." Maddie hustled him around to the passenger side and helped him heave onto a seat that had more exposed springs jabbing his backside than upholstery padding it.

She raced around to the driver's side and piled in. "Put this on." She thrust a brightly striped poncho and a floppy straw hat into his lap, then threw the jalopy into gear.

They peeled out—or more like jerked in fits and starts off the shoulder and onto the pavement. Traffic was blessedly sparse on the two-lane county road this time of day, and only one vehicle—a zippy little sports car—darted around them, the driver shooting them a nasty glare. Thankfully, Chris had his head ducked, putting on the poncho, and his arm was up, partially covering his face. He only caught the passing scowl from the corner of his eye. Hopefully, that was one potential witness who wouldn't be able to identify them if he was ever asked.

"Where on earth did you come up with this crate? And these clothes?" He sniffed the poncho he'd thrown on and wrinkled his nose. "What is that smell?"

"Goat, no doubt."

She chuckled as they widened the distance between

them and pursuit at a whopping thirty miles per hour, as far as Chris could tell by the wavering speedometer. How long this tub would continue to run at all was anybody's guess.

"I never made it to that convenience store," Maddie continued. "There are some interesting residences tucked away in this hilly area. I came upon a rickety trailer house set off by itself in a small coulee, and the kindly, goat-raising inhabitants were happy to sell me this truck and these clothes for more than what they were worth. But now I'm broke, so I'm glad that wallet of yours is still plump and sassy."

Chris frowned. "Don't you think the cops will happen upon the same house as they comb the area?"

"Trust me, these folks aren't the kind to tell the cops anything if they can help it. I expect they'll play dumb, but even if they don't, we need to ditch this jalopy and our goofy disguises before much time passes. Where to, Sherlock?"

"You're asking *me?*"

"You're the man with the plan, aren't you? Isn't that what you were doing while you were sitting on your backside waiting for me?"

Chris twiddled his fingers against the door's armrest, a chunk of padded rubber that looked as if a goat had taken bites out of it. "I pieced together a few things."

He told her about his conclusions regarding the date, time and place for the next drug shipment, and she agreed without argument. A major milestone.

"But," he continued, "unless we can find someone in authority willing to take our word against a state representative's, what we know is useless. The key to digging ourselves out of this hole will be to determine if we have any contacts out there we can trust. But first, how about we round me up a wheelchair so I have a little more mobility? I know just where we might find one—if you can get us there in this thing."

"Bonita Bates's house?" Maddie frowned. "Sure, she might have an extra wheelchair we could borrow or buy. She might even like us enough and resent the government sufficiently to keep our visit quiet. That's a big 'if,' considering why we're wanted. But you in a wheelchair isn't exactly going to be inconspicuous."

"Neither is me limping like my left foot is on fire—which it is, by the way. We don't need to ditch our disguises, just change what they are. Then we need to rattle some cages."

"The Dishonorable Representative's?" She glanced at him with raised eyebrows.

"Jess and his mystery bodyguard and their pet DEA agent. But that's an incomplete set. There's someone else lying in the weeds, and we need to know who it is. Let's see if we can flush out whomever in the local police force or federal agency ordered the assault on us at the motel with sirens blaring."

Maddie clucked her tongue. "Risky business. I like it! But how do you intend to accomplish this without getting ourselves caught or dead?"

Chris chuckled. "For our purpose of the moment, my wallet also contains an item handier than mere cash. Listen closely, Grasshopper."

ELEVEN

"Get on in here. Hurry!" Bonita motioned urgently for Maddie and Chris to cross the threshold into her house.

Maddie stepped forward, but Chris stuck out his arm, blocking her path. What now? She sent him a dark look, but he paid her no attention. His focus was upon their potential hostess.

"You do know who you're inviting into your home, don't you?" Chris said to the woman.

"Not a couple of murdering traitors." She snorted. "But I figure you folks are on the trail of the ones who are."

Maddie crossed her arms over her chest. "You know that how?"

Bonita lifted her chin. "You treated me more than fair when you didn't have to do it. That's not the character of greedy graspers hand-in-glove with drug dealers. But this mess you're in sure smells like some weasel in authority has set you up to take the fall. I know how this works. Hector taught me all about conspiracies."

Maddie met Chris's quick glance. Some might figure this woman certifiable—except she'd stated nothing less than the truth in this case.

"Now quit dolly-waddling on my doorstep," the older woman said, "and get inside where the neighbors can't take a closer look at you goat-farm rejects." She sniffed audibly in the direction of Chris's poncho, then whirled her wheelchair and scooted deeper into her kitchen.

Maddie helped Chris enter and then shut the door behind them. For the first time since guiding that rattletrap truck through city back streets, half expecting police company on their tails at any moment, a deep breath filled her lungs. She savored the cooking smells in the air, then let the oxygen out slowly.

"You're hurt." Bonita motioned toward Chris's leg.

He offered a half smile. "I took a tumble."

"Sprained or broken?"

"We think sprained," Maddie said.

Bonita pursed her lips. "Go on in the living room and get that foot up. The best thing for a sprain is rest."

"This isn't a good time for us to kick back," Chris said. "We were hoping you might have an extra wheelchair we could buy from you."

"Happens I do, but you can borrow it at no charge."

Chris shook his head. "With the kind of trouble we're in, it's hard to say if we'll be able to return it to you or what damage it could suffer."

Maddie studied the whorls on the plaster ceiling. Bonita didn't know the half of it, and it was for the best that she didn't. She and Chris had no idea what shape *they'd* be in after tonight, either. Chris's plan was a long shot, but since she didn't have a better idea, she was going to go along with it. While Chris dickered on the wheelchair—Bonita trying to sell her chair for little or nothing to help with "the cause," and Chris insisting on a fair price—Maddie took stock of their surroundings. She sniffed the air again and eyed the slow cooker on the counter. Her mouth watered.

"Tell you what," she broke into the negotiations, "you split the difference between what Chris is offering and what you are asking, throw in a couple of platefuls of whatever you've got cooking, and help us put together better disguises than what we're wearing right now—"

"At least better smelling," Chris broke in.

Maddie shot him a glare, and he answered with his lethal grin that sent her heart careening around her rib cage like a pinball. She forced the unruly organ back into place and turned her attention toward their hostess. "Help us come up with something that will pass without a second glance in public, and we'll consider it a good deal."

"Done!" Bonita pronounced. "Grab some plates out of the cupboard, and we'll put our thinking caps on over some of the best chili you've ever tasted in all your born days."

Three hours later, Maddie's gullet was still warm from the potency of that chili, but Bonita hadn't been joking when she said it would be the best she'd tasted. Spicy-hot food didn't bother her…or Chris, either, apparently. The guy was humming under his breath and tapping a jaunty rhythm against Bonita's scuffed leather overnight bag on his lap as Maddie wheeled him toward the check-in counter of a major chain hotel in the heart of downtown Laredo.

From Bonita's house they'd called in a reservation, and then donned their disguises as a married couple several decades older than their real ages—which included salt-and-pepper wigs, spectacles with glass lenses and the addition of fake dentures for Chris in order to alter the shape of his too-public face. Their hostess had known of a costume outlet offering cheap prices that would help them conserve the rest of Chris's cash for other vital equipment that might not be so reasonably priced.

Costumed and with wheels under Chris, they grabbed a ride downtown in the handicapped accessible mini-bus taxi that normally picked Bonita up for her shopping expeditions. They left the rattletrap truck under a tarp in their hostess's backyard. Maddie had told her to junk it and get what she could for the scrap metal. Then their chili-meister hostess had insisted the broken-down vehicle was more than enough payment for the wheelchair Chris rode.

They neared the hotel desk, and Maddie's chest constricted. Her toes protested the snug fit of Bonita's granny-style loafers that squeaked faintly on the marble floor. She was probably walking like that shoes-too-tight Special Agent Blunt. The sacklike dress swish-tickled against Maddie's calves, annoying her to no end, and the quilt batting strapped around her middle itched her sides. Minor inconveniences. This outrageous plan had better work like a greased turbine, or the hotel staff was not going to be pleased about cleaning up after their dead bodies. She brought Chris's chair to a halt at the counter.

The statuesque lady behind it beamed at them. "May I help you?"

"Reservation for Chris Morse," Chris answered and produced from his wallet the item he'd promised was better than cash—a credit card in the name he had given.

The desk clerk accepted the card and began processing the check-in.

Sweat prickled Maddie's scalp under the mesh of the wig. That card had better be good. He said he'd used it during a recent story when he needed to travel undercover, and he didn't think his television station had canceled it yet. Didn't *think*? As if that was a sure thing? She ground her teeth together.

"Sign here, and you're good to go, sir." The clerk laid the charge slip on the counter, along with a pen.

Chris reached up awkwardly from his seat in the chair and scribbled on the signature line. Maddie's pulse rate slid back toward normal as they headed for the elevator with their key cards. A couple of minutes later, they were in a hotel room, but the fifth floor and a dead bolt were no comfort when they were about to invite their would-be killers inside.

Maddie kicked off the tormenting loafers and breathed thanks for soft carpet beneath her bare soles as she strode to the window and drew the curtains shut on gathering dusk. Chris rolled up to the desk and then reached into his mouth. Maddie raised her eyebrows. He pulled out the fake dentures, rolled his jaw and smacked his lips.

"Uncomfortable as my shoes?" She laughed.

"Tell me about it." He opened the leather bag on his lap. On the desktop, he laid out the three small, motion-activated camcorders they'd purchased at an electronics store.

"Do your thing, Ms. Communications Officer," he told Maddie.

"My pleasure." She sat down and got to work programming the cameras and syncing them to transmit to a hand-held touch screen about the size of an iPad.

If she was the type to be made nervous by someone watching over her shoulder, she'd be ready to bop Chris. He leaned so close his breath ruffled the wig hairs against the side of her neck. Tingles cascaded to her toes. On second thought, maybe she should at least snap at him—get him to back off. She enjoyed his nearness way too much for her own good—or his. How could there be any future for them, even if they outlived this mess? But, oh, how her heart longed to go there.

"You really believe they'll make a play for us in a public hotel?" At least her voice came out sounding halfway normal, though her throat was a little tight from her battle against raging attraction.

"They've got to be desperate to shut us up," Chris answered. "They'd be fools not to grab any opportunity.

Yes, I think we can count on catching Ramsey's mug on-screen—him and someone else. Probably whoever is the mole among the feds or the local PD."

"I'd be in favor of getting some good shots of the very *special* Agent Blunt."

Chris chuckled. "You really didn't hit it off with him, eh?"

"To put it mildly. He all but accused me of complicity, and the questions he asked about my dead fellow rangers were downright insulting. If my leg hadn't been in traction in a hospital bed, I might have tossed him out of the room on his ear. But why are you so sure Ramsey won't handle this by himself?"

"With you in the equation?" Chris snorted. "Jess's pet DEA agent would need to have his head examined to take us on alone."

Maddie chuckled. "I appreciate the compliment. My second favorite candidate for Ramsey's helper would be Jess's mystery sidekick. A few shots of him attempting murder would connect the representative directly to illegal activity."

"Exactly why I'm ninety-nine-point-nine percent sure it won't be him. Those two will insist on keeping a deniable distance and order their lackeys into the field."

"Jess and his muscle-bound shadow are rat-hole cowards." Maddie turned and handed Chris one of the programmed cameras. "But they have no way of knowing that we've already identified them—or at least the representative."

Not the bodyguard. How could she even begin to verbalize the dread that fell on her at the memory of the man's face hovering over her—the click of a round chambering in a handgun as she lay helpless?

Her grin melted. Who was that man she'd seen in the

desert? How could Chris have missed running into him? If they weren't in cahoots, why was Chris still alive? For that matter, why was *she* still alive? What had stopped the mystery man from pulling the trigger? All unanswerable questions—so far. But that could change with the chain of events they were initiating tonight. It *had* to change, or they might as well stop fighting the inevitable death and dishonor.

She ducked her head and went back to work at the desk.

"No worries," Chris said. "As soon as we get to a computer somewhere, it won't take me long to find out the name of that Popeye clone. But for our purposes right now, it's best if Jess and Popeye Two keep the illusion of anonymity."

Maddie frowned. If Chris had some connection to Representative Jess's bodyguard then he was doing a stellar job of behaving otherwise. Oh, how she wanted to believe that another person could have survived the attack who was not a party to it.

"Once we identify whoever else is in the picture—literally—" Chris wagged the camera in the air "—we can make an informed decision on who might be open and interested in our film and what we have to say about the situation, without shooting or locking us up."

"If anyone." Maddie sniffed.

"Oh, ye of little faith." Chris tsked with his tongue.

A pang struck Maddie's stomach. He'd spoken flippantly, but the truth hurt. She had too many reasons to doubt for faith to be more than a flicker in her soul.

Biting back a sharp answer, Maddie rose. She took one of the cameras and positioned it where Chris suggested on a shelf in the television cabinet. Another one went in the bathroom on the counter, camouflaged inside an unzipped shaving kit. They left the last one on the desk, facing the room's entrance.

"We should easily catch faces on tape," Chris pronounced with a nod. "Along with some nice action shots of our attackers while they're pumping bullets at us. Now it's time to make a fateful phone call." He held out his hand.

Maddie pursed her lips then tossed the handset to Chris. She'd be good with *fateful* as long as this scheme didn't take a nasty turn toward *fatal*.

"I have no idea what you're talking about," Agent Clyde Ramsey snarled into Chris's ear. "What meeting at a paper plant?"

"Don't play innocent with me, Ramsey," Chris said into the phone. He checked to make sure the recorder hooked up to the receiver was working properly. It was. He bottled a smile. "I *saw* you, and Jerrard *heard* you."

"If you're so sure it was me, why don't you turn yourselves in and tell the arresting officers all about it?"

Chris's stomach knotted. Was this clown really going to play hardball and call their bluff? One way to find out.

"If I hang up without getting satisfaction from you, that's exactly what we'll do, and take our chances with the law. That is, after I've pulled in a few favors and gone on television with our story. I'm sure Fernando Ortiz and your boss on this side of the border will be pleased with the publicity."

A soft hiss of breath answered him. *Gotcha!*

"What is it you want?" The words were low and tight.

"Get with whoever is in charge of your smuggling outfit in the States and authorize a payoff for Madeleine Jerrard and me to go away. We want five million dollars wired to an off-shore account and a flight on a private jet to Rio, with resident visas waiting for us on the other end. And be quick about it."

"You don't want much, do you?" Ramsey varnished his tone with a thin sneer.

"Pocket change, and you know it. We're tired of hanging out in the wind, targets for assassination or arrest. We want to get you out of our hair as much as you want us out of yours."

Silence blanketed the air for several heartbeats.

"What's the bank account number for the wire transfer?"

"Not so fast, Ramsey. We want to see you face-to-face—*mano a mano*. You are going to personally accompany us on the flight to Rio, and Ms. Jerrard will have her eye on you the entire way so there is no double-cross."

The DEA agent spat a foul word. "I'll have to get back to you on the arrangements. Might take an hour or two. What phone number should I use to call you back?"

Chris chuckled, the knot in his chest easing. So far, so good. "Don't play me for an idiot. Trying to get a fix on us by our phone number? We'll call you in *one* hour, not a minute longer, and you'd better have the arrangements all set." He jammed the handset into its cradle and looked up at Maddie.

A smile toyed with the edges of her lips, but she shook her head. "You know we're playing patty-cake with a nest of rattlers, don't you?"

"Let's get ready to bite them back."

She jerked a nod, and they swung into action.

An hour later, Chris got on the phone with Ramsey again.

"Are we good to go?" he asked the DEA agent.

"We're on board at this end. You two disappearing is a good deal for us, too. It'll take some of the heat off. The

Jackson murder case will be considered solved even though the perps got away." Ramsey chuckled.

"The shooter was you, I presume?"

"I don't shoot and tell." The smugness in the reply was as good as a confession. "Let's just say the guy's conscience had been working overtime, and we were a little nervous what he might blab if the right buttons were pushed."

"So you rushed right over to your partner's house and shut him up forever before we could get to him. I guess in your line of work it pays to have no conscience."

"Don't go all self-righteous, Mason, when you're boarding the gravy train with me." The steam in the snarl could have shriveled a cactus.

"Just trying to survive." *Touchy, touchy,* he mouthed to Maddie, who sat in a guest chair close enough to hear every word of the conversation.

Her scowl lightened the least bit. If he were Ramsey and caught a glimpse of the look in the eyes of a woman as dangerous as Madeleine Jerrard, he'd run so fast his legs could hardly keep up with him. This slick sellout wasn't that smart.

"We'll meet you at dawn in the airport terminal," he told the DEA agent, "only we won't look like us, but don't worry. Just stand around in the terminal twiddling your thumbs, and *we* will find *you.* Then we fly pronto, so have the plane gassed up and ready."

"Sure, sure. Anything else you want, your majesty?"

"Har-de-har. Be there. Be alone. And soon enough you'll get your wish to be rid of us."

"I'm counting on it." The agent broke the connection.

Chris looked at Maddie. "Hanging up like that, he must be pretty confident he got a read on our location."

"I told you, Mason, digital traces are almost instantaneous. The hour we gave them between phone calls gave him plenty of time to set up the equipment."

"Then we can expect company shortly. There's no way they won't take this opportunity to silence us permanently for the cost of a few ounces of lead."

"Roger that."

Chris stifled a chuckle at the crisp military talk emerging from the lips of one who resembled a gray-haired candidate for the Red Hat Society. She was awfully cute, even as a senior citizen.

Would he get the opportunity to know Maddie at that age?

He shoved the foolish question away. He hadn't forgotten his personal commitment to keep his head on straight, even though his resolve had turned as slippery as a greased eel. But even if they survived this mess, and Maddie was no longer on his off-limits list, the chances were slim to none that their relationship would develop into something lasting. She might be attracted to him, but she couldn't bring herself to wholly trust him. No relationship could survive such suspicion.

He turned his wheelchair away from her. "Let's get ready to be murdered."

TWELVE

The odor of cleaning solutions tingled in Maddie's nostrils as she hunkered on her haunches next to Chris's wheelchair between a housekeeping cart and a rack full of towels. Popping the lock on the door of this closet hadn't taken much finesse, but she wasn't crazy about their surroundings. Too confined. Only one exit. But there was no way to change their location now, even if she had an idea for a better one.

Chris stared at the receiver screen clutched in his hands, then let out a hoot like he was jeering at a sports play. Maddie jerked then huffed. Somebody was having way too much fun.

"All riiiight, maggots!" He snickered. "Come on in with guns blazing."

Maddie studied his profile. There wasn't much light where they hid in the housekeeper's closet down the hall from their hotel room, but the bluish glow from the monitor painted Chris's feral face with an eerie patina as if he were some manic Highland warrior.

She returned her attention to the view on the screen that had him mesmerized. The camera on the desk was picking up movement at the door. The resolution was grainy at best, so it hadn't been able to show what must have happened seconds ago—the unlatching of the dead bolt with a neat turn from a powerful magnet applied on the other side of the entrance. Now the door crept open and a dark figure was removing a high-tech device from the keycard slot.

None of the small sounds that must have accompanied these actions carried through the audio feed from the unit on the desk, the only one Maddie had left active for audio. All they heard was the nattering, clapping and laughter from a popular late-night talk show on the television.

"Yessss!" Chris's hiss raised the hairs on the back of Maddie's neck as much as the sight of a second man slinking through the door.

She held her breath. Who was he? The camera shot wasn't yet good enough to tell. The first man moved past the entrance to the bathroom and came within identification range of the camera on the desk. Ramsey. Definitely.

The DEA agent crept closer, and the camera near the television began to pick him up, as well. In a separate window on the receiver screen, the second camera displayed an awesome shot of Ramsey's face, lips peeled back in a toxic snarl. The guy must smoke like a tire factory to have such yellow teeth. In a gloved hand, he trained a gun fitted with a fat silencer on the back of the inflatable head and torso propped in a guest chair in front of the television set.

The second man stopped beside the door to the bathroom. He must hear the shower water running—exactly as planned. The gun-toting conspirators exchanged nods. Chills shimmered through Maddie. How weird to be able to watch from the outside when a bullet is about to tear through what they think is a live target—you!

Ramsey opened fire on the dummy in front of television, and the TV noises abruptly stilled amidst the sound of the shattering screen. The second man rammed through the bathroom door and popped shots toward the inflated figure standing under the *cold* shower—hot water would have steamed up the camera lens. Killer number two's face sprang into sharp focus, and a sour taste entered Maddie's mouth. How disappointing.

"That's not Special Agent Blunt," Chris pronounced.

"No, unfortunately. I've never met this guy before, but we *have* seen him."

"The agent standing next to Blunt during Jess's news broadcast."

"How do we find out his name?"

"Leave that to me, Grasshopper."

Curses carried to them through the receiver. Ramsey had checked the status of his supposed kill and had discovered he'd assassinated a blow-up doll wearing a man's blond wig. The second killer emerged from the bathroom indulging in similar slang.

"I popped a mega-balloon," the man said to Ramsey.

"Me, too. They didn't trust us and cleared out. Let's do the same. We'll have to take them when they show up at the airport."

"If they do." The rogue FBI agent snorted.

"We can always hope. The boss is not going to be happy."

The pair trotted from the room and closed the door after themselves with an audible *thunk*.

Maddie heaved out a long breath. "Too bad they didn't mention Jess's name, rather than the generic 'boss' terminology."

Chris chuckled. "We lassoed the moon, and you want the stars, too? In good time. All in good time."

"You really enjoy this cloak-and-dagger stuff." She awarded him a wide-eyed glare as she rose from her haunches to a standing position.

"You don't?" His eyebrows lifted.

"Gives me the willies. This is creepy CIA-type junk.

We rangers don't skulk around in closets. We face our enemies."

Chris sighed as he tucked the video-receiver screen into its carrying pouch that he'd attached to his belt. "Before this is over, you're all too likely to get your wish."

"Shh!" Maddie gripped his arm and stared toward the closet door, pulse hammering in her throat.

The lock clicked and the door handle turned. Was Chris's prophecy about to come true?

Maddie's gut clenched. If she'd spent hours dreaming up worst-case scenarios, she couldn't have arrived at a more vulnerable location for them in a face-off. No way to retreat and no room to maneuver. Why hadn't she protested when he insisted they take cover in an enclosed space?

Her muscles gathered into combat mode. If Ramsey and his sidekick were beyond that door, quick thinking and quicker reflexes might be all that stood between them and sudden death.

Busted!

Chris stared up into a pair of angry brown eyes. They belonged to a Hispanic man dressed in neatly pressed slacks and a button-down shirt with a name tag pinned to it that said Manager.

"Guests reported voices coming from this closet," the manager said. "I could not imagine such a thing to be true. Who are you, and what are you doing here? Stealing supplies?" The man's gaze scanned them up and down, then performed a rapid sweep across the contents of the closet.

Maddie shifted her stance, and Chris folded his fingers around her forearm. The sinews beneath his fingertips were taut as guitar strings.

"Not thieves, sir," Chris answered. "Frivolous guests

playing a rather ill-advised game of hide-and-seek. We apologize for causing trouble."

The manager's dark brows snapped together. "You're registered guests?"

"Certainly. If you will check your records, you will find a Chris Morse on your register."

"Hmm." The man frowned. "How did you get in here? The supply closet is kept locked."

"Ah, I'm afraid my—er, nurse—" he glanced up at a stone-faced Maddie "—is quite handy with such things. A hobby of hers."

The manager's eyes darkened. "I'm calling security." He swiped a two-way radio from a tooled leather belt.

"While you do that, would you mind if we stepped out? I'm suddenly feeling claustrophobic."

Chris released his hold on Maddie's arm, and she took her cue as if they'd planned the next move. They were quite a team if she'd only admit it. Pushing his wheelchair forward, she gave the manager no option but to retreat or be run over. The man scrambled backward, barking commands into his walkie-talkie.

Without missing a beat, Maddie marched the wheelchair up the hall away from their room. *Good girl. Lead pursuit away from that area.*

The last thing they needed was for the bullet holes in the walls and furnishings to be discovered before they were clear of the hotel. The evidence of foul play would bring the cops swarming, and it wouldn't take them long to run a few prints and find out exactly who had occupied that room. Then the dog-and-pony show would really begin with multiple law enforcement agencies and media-types converging. Maybe the extra publicity for the hotel would make up for the cost of repairing their hotel room.

"Wait! Stop!" The manager's voice followed their hasty retreat, and then his running feet did the same.

Maddie halted.

The tone of voice alone sent a shiver up Chris's spine. It must have done the same for their pursuer because his footsteps no longer trailed them as Maddie's pace accelerated. She whipped the wheelchair around a corner, and Chris's body wrenched sideways. If not for a steely grip on the chair arms, he would have pitched end over end onto the carpet. He righted himself and let out a muted whoop.

A growl of strangled laughter answered him. "Incorrigible," she muttered. "Completely incorrigible."

"Did someone say my name?" he quipped back.

At the end of the hall a set of elevator doors were starting to close behind departing passengers. His driver took off at a full-out run, and speed turned the gaudy hotel carpet psychedelic beneath his chair wheels. She whirled the chair, nearly tossing him out onto his face again, and rammed an arm between the doors just as they would have gone shut. They hissed open, and Chris found himself yanked backward into the cubicle.

"Aren't we trapping ourselves in here?" He shot her a questioning glance.

"Hush and take lessons. This is my op now." She jammed her thumb against the button for the sixth floor. They began to ascend.

"Going up?"

Her fingers danced over the entire keypad, lighting every button.

"Heading down to the lobby stands an excellent chance of landing us straight into the arms of security. We'll have to play hide-and-seek for real now. Evasive maneuvers."

"Excellent thinking."

She answered with a begrudging grunt. The elevator

door *dinged* open, and Chris tightened his hold on the chair arms as they whooshed from the box and up the hall at a brisk trot.

"Heading for the stairwell?"

"The one move they won't anticipate with you in a wheelchair."

"Yes, but I'm in this thing for a reason."

"I'll have to help you hobble down one floor."

"Down?"

"Roger that. We need go back to our room to recover the recording of that telephone conversation with Ramsey and those camcorders before the cops swarm the place. I figure we have a brief window of time when the room we rented will be the last place anyone will look for us."

"I agree we need the recording of the phone conversation, but why recover the cam—" Comprehension halted the words on his tongue.

Yes, the video of the attempted murders was recorded on the receiver device in the pouch at his waist, but in order to bring the perpetrators to justice, rather than send them scurrying out of the country, it was essential that they not realize they'd been caught on camera. Maddie's brain cells had one up on him this time.

They arrived at the stairwell without meeting anyone. Chris struggled to his feet and balanced on one foot while Maddie folded up the wheelchair and tucked it under one arm. She flung the other arm around his waist, and he gripped her around the shoulders. The descent took forever, step by painful step. They arrived at the landing on the fifth floor with him panting and her breathing hard.

"Sorry I'm such dead weight for you." He grimaced at her and leaned against the wall while she unfolded his chair.

"I don't appreciate your terminology. It's my job to see

to it that neither of us gets dead. Now take a load off, and wait for me to return for you." She pointed to the wheelchair.

Scowling, Chris plunked into the chair. Ornery, bossy female. His glance took in her feet. Lovely feet. Not dainty—too big for that—but gracefully formed. "They're bare."

"What?" She shot him a sharp look as her hand gripped the doorknob.

He pointed, and she looked down then rippled both sets of elegant toes.

Her gaze took on the barest hint of humor. "No one ever said you were a slouch in the observation department. I couldn't stand those shoes pinching my feet. I'll grab the electronics from our room, but the torture devices can stay behind. If I'm not back in two minutes flat, do whatever you need to do to get yourself and that video out of this hotel."

"You'll be back."

She jerked a nod at him and was gone. Chris waited, listening. The distant *clomp-clomp* of heavy strides and sounds of sharp voices, muffled and indistinct, carried to him over the whoosh of his pulse in his ears. None of the noises came from floor five outside the stairwell door.

Please, God, give Maddie clear sailing, and bring her back to me swiftly and safely.

He twiddled his fingers against the chair arms. The two minutes had stretched into at least five. Call him insubordinate, but he wasn't budging. Maddie *had* to return to him. Any other outcome was unacceptable.

A feminine scream rent the air, then abruptly stilled. Chris's heart attempted a flying leap out his mouth. That sound *had* come from the fifth floor. Sharp pains shot up his arms, and he looked down. The bones of his hands stood out white beneath his skin as he clutched the arms of the chair. He willed his fingers to unclench.

A patter of running feet approached the stairwell. Friend or foe? Chris's gaze raked the area for a potential weapon. He surged from the chair, snatched the fire extinguisher from its case on the wall and raised it over his head. Saving the situation—and Maddie—was up to him now. A ferocity he'd never known swept through him. No one was going to hurt Madeleine Jerrard if he could help it.

A female figure surged through the door and plowed into him, slamming him into the wall. Fiery pain speared up his injured leg, and he lost his hold on the fire extinguisher. The woman caught the plummeting canister in the crook of one arm an instant before it would have clattered to the floor. She gazed up at him with raised eyebrows and a bemused grin.

"Good idea, but if you want to clobber someone you need to stand to one side of the door, not in front of it."

"Maddie! I thought something happened to you. I heard—"

"—the assistant manager's scream. Thumbnail version, while I was in the bathroom collecting that camcorder, someone came in. I hopped into the bathtub and hid behind the bullet-torn curtain. Thankfully, I'd shut off the water, but man, that tub was cold on the bottoms of my bare feet. I heard a female voice muttering about her boss getting all worked up over a pair of old-fogey toilet paper thieves, and then a sharp gasp, then silence. Evidently, the bullet-hole carnage froze her in shock. I couldn't wait for her to call for help, so I popped out from behind the Swiss cheese curtain, and there she was, staring straight at me. She let out one shriek at my sudden lunge in her direction and melted onto the carpet in a stone-cold faint."

Maddie set the fire extinguisher down and shoved their

black overnight case into his arms. "I got everything and then some." She flashed a thin, rectangular object in his face. "Now the assistant manager's master key card is going to get us out of this joint by accessing the kitchen through the Employees Only service elevator. I doubt the cooks will do more than frown at a pair of senior citizens taking a shortcut, and I double doubt the kitchen staff has been alerted to watch for escaping toilet-paper thieves."

A long breath gusted from Chris, and his muscles turned to Silly Putty. They might actually get out of there in one piece—minus handcuffs. He sank onto the wheelchair seat. Maddie pulled open the stairwell door and dragged the chair through it. She whipped him around, and Chris glimpsed a few people gathered outside their rented room. From the uncertainty of their milling, they were likely hotel guests who'd heard the scream.

"Call 9-1-1," a man said to someone else.

None of them spared Maddie and him a glance as she wheeled his chair sedately up a hallway perpendicular to the crisis. The late hour was such that the passage was empty. Maddie whisked him to the staff service elevator and swiped the assistant manager's card. Chris held his breath as the elevator door whooshed open, but it, too, was blessedly empty. The hour was late for housekeepers to be riding up and down—even rather late for much room service to be going on, though the bar and supper club on the first floor were likely doing booming business.

"Punch in the button for the kitchen," Maddie directed him, and he complied.

The elevator descended and then the door *dinged* open on the muted pandemonium of a busy restaurant kitchen. Surprised faces and a few dark glances followed them as they glided through the area, but no one seemed inclined to interrupt their tasks to question a pair of senior citizens taking a shortcut to the back door. Apparently, Maddie was right; the cooks and waitstaff had not been made aware that gray-haired toilet-paper thieves were on the loose in the building. Chris stifled a grin.

At last, they burst free of the hotel into a back alley ripe with kitchen garbage. He pinched his nose shut as Maddie trotted them clear of the stench and onto the sidewalk. Traffic on the street was steady but not brisk.

"I hope you have a good idea about where we can go to ground," she said, "until we decide who to approach with what we've got."

Chris stroked his chin. "In good conscience, we can't involve Bonita further."

"Agreed. Besides, it's unwise to keep returning to the same location. We're bound to get caught that way."

He hugged the leather case containing the cameras to his chest. "Hail us a cab that will take us to a public telephone. I'm going to call in a major favor that I've left dangling out there for a life-and-death situation. I guess this is it."

"No kidding, Sherlock."

Chris clamped his lips shut. He'd hold off as long as possible on telling her who he meant to call. When she found out, her suspicions of him would be confirmed, and he'd be rated the biggest louse on the planet. He might not even live long enough to explain.

THIRTEEN

"**W**hy didn't you think to warn me *before* I climbed into this limo that your super-contact swooping in to save us is *David Greene?*" Bile burned the back of Maddie's throat.

She glared at Chris, who sat with his face pointed toward the panel of tinted glass that separated them from the chauffeur. Could the driver hear what the passengers said? If so, he was getting an earful.

"The spoiled brat of an oil magnate *murdered* his girlfriend and hasn't been charged with a thing. Some savory company you keep!"

No wonder she'd had the jitters about getting into the long white vehicle that showed up for them at the all-night convenience store. At the time, she felt she didn't have any choice but to trust the man who sat beside her, but now that she'd badgered their benefactor's identity out of him, a bad case of second thoughts didn't begin to describe her reaction.

Throbbing fingers of heat spread through her rib cage. She'd been right to cling to her suspicions about Chris. The burn spread upward and stung the backs of her eyes. Why did being proved right tempt her toward tears? She ought to be pleased that her judgment was sound, even if the same couldn't be said of her heart. And why didn't

Chris say anything? Couldn't defend himself, that's why. Her hands balled into fists. Anyone who could place a call to a murdering snake and have said reptile's limo come right out from his Laredo estate and pick them up within minutes couldn't be on the same planet as *trustworthy*.

Chris turned his head toward her, expression stoic in the soft glow of a thin overhead transom light. Or was that a hint of sorrow in the slight downturn of his mouth? Too bad. If she wasn't determined to stay out of jail long enough to nail the hides of certain government coyotes to the wall, she'd call a halt to this vehicle and walk away right now.

"Good thing you're not a dragon, or I'd be fried to ashes," Chris said. "I was half expecting to be throttled by now."

"Don't think the idea hasn't crossed my mind."

Chris winced. "I can't control what you want to believe about me, but don't believe everything you hear in the media."

"Huh? Amazing statement coming from a media icon."

She stuck her nose inches from his. It was the only way she could read his eyes in this dimness. The blue depths were hard and earnest, but a little desperate, too. Or was it guilty? Her stomach soured.

"Do you think David believes what he's heard about *us?*" Chris's question emerged bold and staccato.

"Are you telling me that you know for a fact that Greene *didn't* kill that poor woman?"

"I'm telling you there's more to the story."

"So now you're a Paul Harvey wannabe?"

"No, Harvey said 'the rest of the story.' I guess that line works in David's case, too. Reserve your judgment until you meet him."

Maddie subsided against the butter-soft leather seat and

crossed her arms tight to her chest. "Too late for that. And who says I want to meet him? What he did was vile."

"Agreed."

"See?" She jabbed a finger in his direction. "You admit he did it. And you admit you're his friend, anyway."

An audible gust of air left Chris's nose, and his hands closed around his kneecaps. "I won't argue with you on either count…neither will he." The final three words emerged in the barest whisper.

Sad words, yes, but flavored with an odd dash of hope. What should she make of that? She rolled her jaw, attempting to form a coherent sentence, but nothing came together. How could her wayward heart flirt with loving anyone who had done enough for a creep like David Greene to make him beholden on the level of harboring nationally wanted fugitives? There would never be enough explanation to make that picture acceptable. No wonder she couldn't decide if she wanted to toss her cookies or toss Chris over the nearest bridge into the Rio.

Maddie turned her face toward the side window and the blackness of night that erased the flat landscape and mirrored her mood. At least they'd left the glare of the city behind. Greene had a ranch somewhere out in the boonies where Chris and she could hide and heal and decide what the next step might be. He was after his precious story, but she was after justice. Okay, so she'd keep on working with him in order to achieve her goal, but that was it. If she was able to turn the tables on him and sweep him into the net with the rest of the traitors, she'd do it. He didn't deserve his big story.

But why did the thought of Chris disgraced and jailed wring her heart like a string mop? A deep ache pulsed between her eyebrows. Muscles up and down her body throbbed—a natural consequence of tumbling top over tail out of a fast-moving car not so many hours ago. Fatigue weighted her limbs, and her empty belly twisted itself into a hard knot. But the food contained in the compact refrigerator in the passenger compartment held no appeal.

She leaned her head back into the plush seat. "How long until we reach this Panhandle ranch of his?"

"We should see it by sunup."

She closed her eyes. Fat chance she could sleep, but she'd try to rest while she didn't have anything else to do. That's how a good soldier behaved—grab downtime when the opportunity came. The vehicle was so soundproof even the hum of tires on tarmac didn't reach her ears. Just Chris's breathing. Soft. Steady.

Her idiot heart prodded her to curl up against him. How long had it been since she'd had anyone just hold her for no reason except comfort? A long time ago. When she was a small child maybe? Her military family had never been extravagant in the hug department. They'd shown love in different ways. Encouragement. Respect. Pats on the back. Maddie hadn't known she missed being held…until Chris. He'd ruined her. The rat. Now she'd always be looking for what she could never have.

God, I don't know how to get through this, loving the man I hate. Please, help me.

It had been nearly forever since she'd asked the Lord for something for herself. Jerrards were trained to be self-sufficient. She didn't know what she'd expected when she reached toward Him with her heart, but this nothingness was probably about what she had coming when her fury over events at the Rio extended to Him, too. A long, soundless sigh exhaled through her entire body, and her muscles went slack. Warm weightlessness enfolded her. Yes, she'd rest a little. Not sleep, but—

"We're here." Chris's voice penetrated Maddie's consciousness, along with his pat on her arm.

She jerked awake and sat up. She'd slept? No doubt for hours. Unbelievable!

Maddie shook herself and peered out the tinted glass window of the limousine. A man's torso blocked her view, and she hissed in a breath. The door opened, and the chauffeur stood back, admitting a rush of warm, mesquite-scented breeze and the blush of dawn dusting the outside world.

"Welcome to Cross D Ranch," he said.

Maddie attempted to extend her limbs to climb out of the car, but her muscles responded with a burst of outrage. A groan left her lips, and a stifled chuckle from Chris teased her ears.

"A bit stiff this morning? Join the club. If I can down a couple more painkillers and get this foot iced and up, I'll be happy as a mustang in tall grass."

Maddie glanced over her shoulder toward Chris's swollen ankle. It hadn't been tended since yesterday morning and must be giving him fits, but he'd never said anything. At least the guy wasn't a whiner. Not that the pain in his ankle had anything on the festering ache in her soul. Desperation time. She *had* to find relief…some resolution between her thoughts and her emotions, or she'd be worthless for the confrontations that lay ahead. But she'd been carted off to the worst possible place to find anything resembling peace of mind.

"If Greene can provide accommodations for folks like us," she said, "I'd be surprised if he can't wrangle medical attention for you. We're still not sure about the extent of the damage—torn ligaments, broken bones, etc."

"We'll be well looked after." Chris spoke with quiet assurance.

By a murderer? Not the kind of help Maddie had the slightest interest in accepting, but she swallowed an angry answer. No point in further protest. They were here now.

Gritting her teeth against another groan, she pulled herself out of the vehicle and took a couple of steps forward. Before them, a long-bodied, single-story ranch house sprawled in sturdy grace across a neatly trimmed lawn. The grass was too green not to be watered regularly, but the irrigation system was well hidden. Nice digs, but within the ordinary range. Not as extravagant as she'd expected for a wealthy man's property.

"You can go on in, ma'am," said the chauffeur from behind her. "We fellows will bunk in the south wing. You can have the run of the north side of the house. I think you'll find everything you need there, except a kitchen. My apologies, but we'll all have to share that room, ma'am."

Maddie turned toward the driver. "Thank y—" Words stalled on her tongue as her gaze collided with his.

The man looked to be in his early thirties. He was of medium height and built sinewy, like a marathon runner. Not classically handsome, but arresting with that square chin, rugged cheekbones and coal-black hair curling around his ears. His piercing eyes were the color of fog on the ocean. She knew that face from frequent media exposure.

"Hi, David." Chris's tall form struggled to win free of the vehicle.

"Good to see you, Chris." Their driver bent and helped his friend into a standing position. "I could wish for better circumstances."

Stock-still, Maddie gaped after them as one man helped the other hobble up the sidewalk, tackle the porch steps and disappear into the house. Neither of them awarded her another word or look. The brisk slap of the screen door after them jerked her out of paralysis.

Fine.

If segregation ruled their stay here, she was more than happy to accommodate. When she was good and ready to plan their next move, she'd have to meet with Chris. They had obtained valuable footage, but using it to best effect would require thought. Hopefully, in the meantime their host would get the hint and vacate the premises. For right now, she needed space to decompress.

Maddie marched into the house and found the north end exactly as the owner had described—everything she needed and then some. Across a bed half the size of Texas, someone had laid out several pairs of jeans, a few T-shirts and some serviceable intimate apparel that would fit her decently. She would have had the willies about the clothes perhaps belonging to the murdered girlfriend, but the tags were still on. A gajillionaire probably had tons of employees he could order out shopping in the middle of the night for surprise guests, but whoever had bought the clothing didn't seem to be around. Good move. The fewer people who met the guests, the better for everyone.

She spent the first hour in a hot, scented whirlpool tub that soaked away the lion's share of her aches and pains. Then she donned a satiny robe and padded up the hall toward the kitchen across carpet that nearly swallowed her bare feet. Male voices were retreating from the shared area, so she pattered over a shiny tile floor to the refrigerator and found the fixings for a massive sandwich, as well as a soda to wash it down.

Cradled in a leather recliner in a Southwestern-themed sitting room, she savored her sandwich in front of a television screen that covered most of the wall. An enormous yawn cracked her jaw, but she shook her head. She'd resist sleep at least until she heard the noon news. She woke up in time for the evening report.

Maddie's and Chris's names were central once more in the anchorman's blather, and speculation was rampant about their nefarious purpose at the Laredo hotel. "Authorities have recently reported that the pair may have left the country."

The concluding statement brought Maddie upright in the lounger. People thought they were gone? Really? How did that happen?

She worked the remote control on the chair—yes, the thing was operated electrically!—and hopped up. Her muscles protested the movement with minimal complaint. Progress toward renewed vigor. She'd need every ounce of strength and sanity she could muster.

A few minutes later, clad in a fresh set of clothes, she followed the sound of masculine voices and chuckles to the kitchen. Dressed in casual clothing similar to hers, the men were seated at a polished mahogany table. Chris had his injured foot up on another chair. The leg below the knee was encased in a walking cast and padded wrap-boot. A pair of crutches rested against the wall nearby. Did Greene have a pet doctor in his pocket, too?

As she entered the room, they ceased talking and their heads turned toward her. She stopped and leaned over the center island on her elbows. "Thanks for the hideaway and the clothes and stuff, too." Under the circumstances, she could be polite to anyone, but that didn't mean she approved of their host.

"You're welcome." The man nodded his head.

That misty gaze would be spooky if it wasn't also gentle. A little wary, though, as if he half thought she might go all kung fu on him.

"She does have a nice smile." Their host looked toward Chris.

"Tons of nice things about her," Chris answered.

After indulging the daydream of herself flying through the air in a screaming karate kick, Maddie sucked in the grin she hadn't known was showing. Tons of nice things? *Hmmph!* What had Chris really been telling this man about her? That she was a suspicious, angry woman? Well, she was, and she hated it, but couldn't change until truth was known.

She hugged herself and cleared her throat. "I see you've had medical attention."

Chris's face took on a guarded look, but their host shrugged with a half smile. "Sometimes it pays to be a quarter Apache. The doc on the reservation will make house calls, and he's not inclined to tell tales."

Maddie nodded. That explained that. "Either of you have any idea why the news would report that Chris and I have left the country?"

The men gazed at each other, wearing blank looks.

"We were faking out the government rats that we wanted to head for South America," Chris said to his buddy. "But they know we didn't leave. They were planning to bury us instead."

Maddie narrowed her gaze on David Greene. "You didn't slip some misinformation to the authorities?"

The man answered with a grimace and a shrug. "My pockets aren't deep enough to buy credibility with the police or the news hounds."

"Great!" She dropped her arms to her sides and turned away. "Another mystery."

Maddie hurried up the hallway toward her bedroom. Tears surged behind her eyeballs like a tide against a dam. Frustration? Maybe. But lots more. So much pain she didn't know what to do with it all. But this was not the time to give in, was it? She'd stood strong so far. She just needed to rein in her emotions a little bit longer.

She reached her room, shut the door, and then stood with her fists clenched, barely breathing. But the surge would be denied no longer. Her chest cavity quivered and shook. Then a high-pitched sob escaped, and the dam crumbled. She stumbled into the bathroom and sat hunched over a box of tissues while the long pent-up flood carried her away.

How long she sat huddled on the commode she couldn't say, but at last the gusher subsided into a trickle. Her head ached, and goopy heaviness filled her chest. These were not cleansing tears, and they weren't over. Not by a long shot. Could a person drown in hopelessness and confusion?

What did she do with these feelings for Chris that persisted against the compelling case for mistrust? How could she honor the memory of her fallen comrades when she longed to love the very man that reason dictated was their betrayer? Why were her tears focused in this moment over Chris and not the loss of her brother, her fellow soldiers and her career? Those things hurt, but not like the slash and burn in her heart of the inevitable future without Chris.

On wobbly, leaden legs, she returned to her bedroom, undressed and crawled between the cool sheets. She'd never been so tired in her life—not from physical exertion, but from the utter aloneness that never abated. If she slept forever and a day, would the nightmare end?

Chris tore his gaze from the computer screen and rubbed his eyes with the backs of his hands. He'd been at this for hours again today—three days, total, since David had taken them in. He was starting to feel halfway human again with rest and good food, but his nerves never quite settled.

Maybe that condition came from being a wanted fugitive. Or maybe he couldn't relax because, with every click of the mouse, he uncovered fresh information on their cast of villains. For instance, the duly elected representative to the Texas state legislature, Donald Jess, was the registered owner and CEO of the Rio Grande Paper Plant. *Surprise! Surprise!* The guy also owned some intriguingly isolated property a few miles from the plant, right along the river. A little research via satellite imagery revealed that a ravine wound around from that river property to the factory, maybe the very ravine in which he and Maddie nearly met their Maker. Nifty little concealed route for transportation of contraband by mule or ATV.

As for the FBI agent who'd helped DEA agent Ramsey shoot up the dummies in the hotel room, Adrian Lesko was his name. That tidbit had been a challenge to unearth. The FBI was protective of agent identities, but Chris took a digital cutout of the man's mug from the internet replay of the interview with Representative Jess. Then face-recognition software dug up an obscure story in an online newspaper that featured Lesko spearheading a local school program to help troubled kids make better choices. *Hah!* The urge to barf nearly overcame him on that one. But the biggest challenge had been discovering the identity of Representative Jess's muscleman, and the truth was definitely stranger than fiction. If the knowledge wasn't so dismaying, he'd be doing a jig. In his mind anyway. His gaze strayed to the cast on his leg, and he shook his head.

No, his problem wasn't the hours at the computer. Research energized him; it didn't unnerve him. Then what was his problem? They were closer than they'd ever been to exposing the entire nest of scorpions. All they needed was a neat little plan to tie it all up.

Maybe that was the hitch. There was no "they." For all

he saw of her, his partner seemed to have dropped out of the quest. Maybe her beef with David was the reason. But he sensed something different, something more—as if she was going down for the third time but didn't dare allow anyone close enough to throw her a life raft. The woman was a case and a half, and he needed to have his head examined for caring so much about her. If he wanted to be honest with himself, had he already lost his battle not to fall in love with her?

On a long groan, Chris rose from the desk chair in David's cavernous office and stretched his arms wide, then rolled the kinks out of his shoulders. A pair of crutches leaned against the desk. He tucked them under his arms and hobbled over to the wide window that looked out on the garden at the back of the house.

David's garden. His haven, he called it. Not the usual vegetable plot. In fact, not much in the vegetable department at all. The man was a fiend for flowers—native wildflowers of Texas. He was an expert, and he liked to tend them himself as he was doing right now on his hands and knees not far from the window, trowel busily transferring granules of what must be fertilizer from a bag onto grass beds growing around spikes of Texas Paintbrush. Chris wouldn't even know that much about the kinds of flora out there, except David had insisted on showing off his rare Albino Paintbrush last evening. Evidently the flower didn't show up white very often.

Oops! And there was another flower that hadn't been showing up very often lately. Correction—cactus. Chris frowned toward the tall, slender figure that stepped into view around the side of the house. Maddie followed a red-brick path into the garden area, looking all too appealing in a pair of designer jeans and a trendy T-shirt. She stepped slowly, gaze fixed ahead, as if she walked in her sleep. Were her eyes puffy, or was he imagining things?

Without conscious direction, Chris's hand rose and pressed against the warm glass. So far, he'd heeded her signals that she wanted to be left alone, but they needed to talk. Ready or not.

Uh-oh! His eyes widened. The collision was inevitable. He could see it coming, but he couldn't do a thing to stop it. If she didn't start paying attention to her surroundings, she was going to trip over David's feet and splat onto her face. When she picked herself up, and saw their host, they could be treated to a confrontation of epic proportions.

He turned from the window and began crutching toward the nearest exit. He'd better get out there. Now!

FOURTEEN

Oomph! The breath jarred out of her body.

One second Maddie was treading the garden walk; the next her nose was up against the bricks. Only trained reflexes, certainly not any lightning-fast awareness, saved her noggin from a severe bruising.

Propped up on her elbows, Maddie gazed over her shoulder. Whose feet did she just trip over? Not Chris's. One of his was encased in a walking boot. These clodhoppers wore scuffed and frayed tennis shoes. That eliminated her homicidal host. Or did it?

David Greene unfolded himself from the ground and rose to stand above her, trowel dangling from one grubby fist. "Sorry about that. Are you all right?" His drawl was all West Texas gentlemanly, and then he offered a hand to help her up. "Oops!" He took the hand back and wiped it on his shabby denims.

She got to her feet without extra help and then grimaced at a tear in the knee of her pants. Both knees stung, but between the edges of the rip a streak of blood showed from a minor laceration.

"I'll live. I've experienced worse."

"I'm sure you have. This being an army ranger must be pretty interesting business."

Not half as interesting as yours, buster. She kept the comment to herself. Chris might be surprised to know she had a few manners. "I didn't know millionaires liked to get their hands dirty."

Okay, very few manners. She hadn't meant the comment quite like it came out. Then again, maybe she had, considering the things she knew about him. Or thought she knew. Nothing about this guy had been what she'd expected.

From the little she'd seen of the man, he was soft-spoken and good-humored. He had surprisingly stodgy taste in music, judging from the classical piano CDs that played occasionally on the other end of the house, but she couldn't fault him as a gracious and thoughtful host. Nor had she glimpsed so much as a rolled joint or a pipe, a bottle of booze or a happy pill on the place. The man who'd strangled his girlfriend had been publicized as a party animal with all the vices the super-rich could indulge in.

This man in grubby jeans grinned and turned toward the plants he'd been working on. "Money can't buy the satisfaction of growing a perfect white *Castilleja indivisa.*"

"A castle-what?"

"A very rare Albino Paintbrush." Greene chuckled and patted a cream-hued flower spreading large petals from a long, leafy stalk. "This entire garden is wildflowers and grasses native to Texas." He spread his arms toward the colorful vista that was his backyard.

Maddie scanned the varied hues that splashed the landscape all the way to the horizon. She'd seen smaller corn fields. This "garden" extended for acres and acres. Many hours these past days had been consumed in wandering the maze of paths and reading the occasional posts that told what was growing here and there. The guy could charge admission and offer a display well worth the cost.

"Do you tend all this yourself?"

"As much as I can." His smile went rueful. "This project is bigger than one person though. Teams come out pretty regularly from arboretums in and out of state. They come to study, and generally they lend a hand. I've also got a yard man that bunks with the other hands at ranch headquarters."

"This isn't headquarters?"

"Naw. This is my getaway cottage. Headquarters is too busy for my taste. Stables and barns and pastures and fields with wranglers coming and going all over the place. The big house sits empty, except for the housekeeper, most of the time."

"Oh." Maddie blinked and gazed off over Greene's shoulder toward clumps of feather-topped grasses waving in the breeze.

What else could she say? It made sense that this guy's idea of a cottage would dwarf most family homes. So why was she standing around making small talk with David Greene? She should walk away, but something held her in place—a need to get a clear read on this man who'd made her grudgingly beholden.

"Go ahead and ask." Weariness, or perhaps resignation, tinged her host's voice.

"Ask what?"

"Did I kill Alicia?"

Heat worked its way up Maddie's neck. Was she that obvious? Apparently so. "I suppose everyone you meet is wondering about that."

Greene walked a few steps away and plunked down on a stone bench. He ran splayed fingers through his thick hair. Whatever he'd been using in his gardening left streaks of a gray substance among the midnight strands. Then he nodded and met her steady look. "It does get old. I wish I knew myself. I mean, there's circumstantial evidence that says I did, but I don't remember. Nobody really seems to *get* what that feels like—not to be sure what happened— how it happened—what I did. Even if it's the worst, it would be nice to *know*."

Maddie studied her host. Greene wasn't much older than she was, but his eyes were ancient. She recognized the haunted, hunted, lonely look from the gaze that stared back at her regularly in the mirror. She fought the urge to press the heels of her hands to swollen eyes she knew betrayed the tears she'd been shedding in fits and starts over the past three days. Why had that abundance of tears not yet eased the knotted mass of pain that weighted her chest like a cancer?

A lump invaded her throat, and she cleared it. "I do get what it's like not to be able to remember events that changed a person's whole world."

The edges of Greene's mouth drooped. "Chris told me a little about it. You were wounded. I was just wasted. My own fault, all of it." He pinched the bridge of his nose and looked away. "The blanks would drive me crazy if Chris hadn't gone out of his way to hunt me down after all the media hoopla and make me listen to the truth."

Maddie's eyebrows climbed up her forehead. "Chris missed his calling as a psychotherapist. He pops that stuff on me all the time, too."

Greene chuckled. "Chris made no attempt to fix me or figure me out or milk a story out of me. The last person I wanted to talk to was a reporter, even if he was an old acquaintance, but he was persistent. Finally I agreed to see him, but to my shock, he didn't want an exclusive interview, though I gave him one later. He just wanted to talk to me about Jesus. Said God wouldn't let up on him until he gave me the chance to meet my Savior. And do you want an even bigger shock? I listened when I never had before."

Maddie sucked in a deep breath. "So that's the big favor he did you?"

"About the biggest there is, don't you think?" Her host's silvery gaze bored into her. "At least now I know I'm forgiven for whatever I did. Chris is a good man. He could never do what they're accusing him of doing…you, either. Not if the half of what Chris tells me about you is true."

"What?" Maddie struggled to process the implication of Greene's words.

This man who might or might not be a murderer acquitted her without knowing her, purely on the basis of Chris's say-so. Such faith in God…in Chris…in her…spoke louder than all the logic-driven suspicions in her head. She should have listened to her heart all along—or the voice of the Holy Spirit, if she'd been able to recognize Him speaking through her heart.

Her knees went weak, and she plunked onto the bench beside a possible murderer without a second thought. Realizations lasered through her mind, shedding light into dark corners.

Of course, Chris had nothing to do with the massacre on the Rio. Of course! He couldn't have. Not that he *couldn't,* but it wasn't in his nature. Why had she not seen something so obvious until this moment? She'd been searching for a scapegoat. Craved one! Someone she could see and touch. Someone solid, not a big black question mark. She couldn't handle not knowing, so she'd made a case out of circumstance and clung to it blindly with all the stubbornness in her natural makeup.

How could she ever face Chris again? How could she not! Pressure squeezed her chest, her throat, her eyeballs. Not again! She couldn't cry more. Not here. Not now.

"Umm. Are you all right?"

David's hesitant words barely registered. A sob gathered like a clenched fist in her windpipe.

Chris gaped as his warrior princess slumped on the bench, hugging herself against muted sobs and scrunched together like she might fly apart if she let go. He'd almost made it to the scene in time to stop whatever had happened, but not quite. Bother the need for these crutches! What had David said to her?

He glared toward his friend, who responded with a shrug and spread hands. "I told her why I owe you more than my life. That's all." David rose and scurried toward him like a man escaping a fire. "She's all yours, man," he said as he hustled past.

Chris swallowed and took a deep breath. Chances were, Maddie's condition made sense only to her, but her comfortless sniffles wrenched his heart right out of his chest. He crutched forward and sank onto the bench near her.

"Hey." He touched her shoulder.

She jerked and peered up at him, cheeks glistening with rivulets of water as if she stood under a shower. "Oh, Chris!"

She lunged toward him, and he wrapped her close. Her whole body shook as she buried her face against his shoulder and raised the water pressure. She must have had this stuff dammed up since the Rio, or maybe even before. Who knew when this stoic woman had cried last? Who cared, as long as she did it in his arms?

Comfort babble flowed from his lips, but he didn't pay much attention to what he said exactly. Hopefully, she wasn't retaining much more than the tone of his voice, because he probably made about as much sense as any lovestruck man with the woman of his dreams curled against him, trusting him with her tears.

Shadows lengthened, but time was of no consequence as he held her, and they rocked together. At last, the sobs tapered into deep, shuddering breaths. Then she lifted her head a little and peered up at him. If raccoon masks were red and encircled bloodshot eyes, she'd be an awfully cute coon. He smiled down at her.

"I'm s-sorry," she hiccuped. "I've been a b-blind-headed fool. I know you didn't sell us out at the Rio. I *know* it in here." She pulled away and pressed a hand to her heart. "And in here." She tapped her forehead. "I still don't know what really happened but—"

"Shh." He pressed a finger to her lips. "We'll figure it out. Maybe it's just as important to realize what *didn't* happen."

A smile quivered at the edges of her lips, and her gaze lightened with…what? Hope? Yes, but something more. Did he dare think it might be the beginnings of love for him? Did he want her love? Yes!

God help him, but it was time to raise the white flag… at least to himself. The battle against his commonsense resolve to remain detached was lost. He wouldn't inform her yet about his glorious defeat. The timing was premature. And besides, he wanted—no, needed—for her to move beyond simple trust and into something stronger. Maybe he could help the process along in another way besides words.

Chris gathered her close and kissed her mouth, her cheeks, her eyelids, the sides of her jaw—and she didn't resist. His heart soared. In fact, she kissed him back, little giggles erupting in place of the sobs. The leftover salt of her tears made a sweet savor on his lips. Finally, they sat quietly, arms around each other, her head resting on his shoulder. If peace were a river, they were happily floating away downstream.

"It's wet," she said.

"What?"

"Your shirt. Soggy as a dishrag."

"You know whose fault that is, right?"

"Yup. Do you mind?"

"Nope. Cry a bucket on me anytime, though I hope it's never me that gives you cause."

She let out a long sigh and sat up. "We have a lot to talk about. A lot to do. We can't afford to waste time cuddling."

"I know." With the tips of his fingers, Chris brushed a lock of golden hair out of her face. "I've been a busy boy these past three days." He told her the connection between Representative Jess and the Rio Grande Paper Plant, as well as what he'd discovered about the FBI agent who'd conspired with DEA Agent Ramsey to kill them at the hotel. "And I found out the identity of our mystery muscleman shadowing Representative Jess. His name is Richard Glick. Does that name ring a bell?"

Maddie shrugged. "No. Should it?"

"Jess hired him as his bodyguard after some much-publicized threats on his life from the Ortiz Drug Cartel because of his position on the Texas Homeland Security and Public Safety Committee."

A mask of grim glee settled over her face. "Hah! Pretty clever to manufacture a bogus threat. Makes them look like champions of justice when they're hand-in-glove with slime."

"You're no slouch on the uptake." Chris chuckled.

"I must be, because none of that tells me why you think I should recognize Glick's name."

Chris took a deep breath. She was going to hate this. "He's a former army ranger."

"He's not!" Maddie leaped to her feet, slicing the air with the edge of one hand. Then she froze on an audible intake of breath and turned slowly back toward him. "No,

I don't mean I doubt you, Chris. I'll never make that mistake again. Word of a ranger. But that's exactly why I'm in such disbelief. Rangers vow to lay down their lives rather than betray their country."

The fire in her gaze had burned away the last vestige of their brief moment of contentment together. He wanted it back, but he dared not press for it. He rose and faced her.

"People are people, and rangers aren't any more infallible than the next mortals when that many dollar signs flash before them."

"But we're supposed to be better than that." Her mouth flat-lined.

Chris ran a hand up and down her arm. Her skin wore a chill even in the late-day warmth. "I know at least one who is better than that."

Her head lowered. "Not in my own strength, though I've been doing pretty well at fooling myself that it's so." She sighed. "I'm nothing without God, and here I've been blaming Him for the evil that people do. How do I make it up to Him?" Her searching gaze lifted to Chris's.

He risked encircling her in an embrace, and she didn't pull away. "His arms are wide open for you and infinitely more welcoming than mine."

Maddie let out a forlorn chuckle. "I guess I need to spend some time getting reacquainted. I think I can handle that. Correction. I think I'll let Him help me with that." She turned her head toward the house. "David's playing those classical piano CDs again. I'm almost starting to like the stuff."

"CDs?" He snickered. "Come with me." Chris grabbed her hand and took a step forward. His ankle protested the weight. Loudly. "Ouch! I keep forgetting these." He reluctantly turned her hand loose and took up his crutches.

She grinned and trod beside him as they went in through

the back door. Coolness enfolded them. Chris led her to a solarium on the south side of the house then let her step into the room first. The stunned look on her face was everything he'd anticipated. David didn't even glance up from the keyboard to acknowledge their presence. His hair was still damp from the quick shower he must have taken while they were in the garden, and he wore clean jeans and a plaid, button-down shirt.

"It's a piece of media-overlooked trivia," Chris said to Maddie, "but Texas's wealthiest oil tycoon could choose to become a concert pianist any day of the week."

David looked up and awarded them a smile but never missed a note. "Do you think my name on the marquee would sell tickets or invite rotten tomatoes?" He offered a lopsided grin, lifted his fingers from the keyboard, and rose. "Did you give her the low-down on your research?" He nodded toward Chris.

"Sure did." Chris found a nearby sofa and sank into it.

Maddie perched next to him, close enough for their shoulders to touch. She really meant it when she said she'd decided to trust him. He suppressed the whoop that filled his windpipe, but couldn't tone down the grin that strained his cheek muscles.

David laughed. "You two patched it up, I see."

A pretty rose color bloomed across her face. "I tried to drown him first. Sorry about losing it in front of you, but thank you for bringing me to my senses."

"No problem." David's eyebrows rose. "Not sure what I said, but glad I could help. Sorry for fleeing the scene, but I've never been good with women and tears. It wasn't me you wanted, anyway."

Chris shot his friend a mock scowl. "If it was, you and I would have had an issue."

Grinning, David threw a punch in the air. "Like I couldn't take you even if you didn't have a gimpy leg?"

"Don't let that little detail stop you from trying." Chris waved a crutch. "Be very afraid."

The men laughed, but Maddie clapped her hands together.

"Men at play are very cute," she said, "but it's time for a serious discussion. We have decisions to make."

She rose, and Chris missed her presence, but the snuggly Maddie had been swallowed by the huntress that now paced the Oriental rug covering a section of the polished hardwood floor.

"Your research is awesome, Chris." She waved a finger at him. "Based on what you've uncovered, we can connect the dots very easily. Too bad we have no way to prove much of it. Anyone in authority—if we could figure out someone to approach—will have a harder time putting the pieces together, and we have nothing concrete tying Representative Jess or Richard Glick to the drug trade."

"We've got Ramsey and Adrian Lesko cold on camera trying to commit murder. That and the recorded phone conversation proves their complicity with the cartel. Surely, they'd cut a deal by rolling over on their bosses."

Maddie shook her head. "They know too well what happens to people who betray the drug runners."

Chris scowled. "Doesn't seem right that betraying the cartel inspires more fear in crooked agents than betraying their country."

"You nailed that irony on the head."

"At least showing the video to someone we can trust—"

"And who would that be?"

He shot her a hard look, and she went still, hands on hips.

"As I was saying," Chris continued, "if we can figure out someone in law enforcement to trust and give them a copy of the video and the phone recording, we will take a huge step toward getting ourselves off the hook."

"How do you see that?"

"Yeah, explain that conclusion," David chimed in. He perched on the end of the piano bench and crossed his arms.

Chris glared from his friend to the woman who drove him crazy in so many ways that he hardly knew which way was up. "They tried to kill us. Clearly we were a threat. Shouldn't that suggest that we might have been framed for the murder of Ramsey's partner?"

"You're thinking like an innocent man, buddy." David shook his head.

"And your meaning is?"

"You're thinking like someone who believes they will actually be considered innocent unless proven guilty. That's not always how these things fly in real life. I found that out firsthand."

Maddie fixed their host with an assessing look. What was going on in that nimble mind of his? Whatever it was, she shook her head and returned her gaze to Chris's.

"Ramsey and Lesko's attempt to murder us in cold blood may put them behind bars, but their action hardly paints us lily-white—either to law enforcement or in the public eye. Crooks fall out among themselves all the time."

Chris picked up one of the scatter pillows from his end of the sofa and chucked it toward the other end.

David let out a sharp chuckle. "Do I detect a little frustration?"

"You two are saying that we went to all that trouble of setting them up at the hotel, and the best we might achieve is to send Ramsey and Lesko to prison along with us."

"Pretty fair assessment." His friend nodded.

"Unacceptable!" Maddie pronounced. "The entire purpose of pursuing this investigation was to expose the real villains of the Rio Grande Massacre. We've done that to our own satisfaction, if no one else's. There's got to be some way to make sure the bad guys lose and the good guys win."

Their host heaved a long sigh, and his gaze fell to his toes.

"Spit it out, David," Chris said. "You've got something on your mind."

Expression unreadable, his friend raised his head and met Chris's gaze. "Answers don't always come how—or even when—we think they should. Maybe God needs you to get out of His way, and let Him take these guys down. Maybe the best thing you can do right now is make sure the good guys don't lose."

"Meaning what?" Maddie's question was sharp-edged, yet her bottom lip trembled, and her eyes were wide as a kid's, anticipating her first day at school.

Did she welcome yet fear some new alternative as much as he did?

"I couldn't live with myself if I didn't do my level best to ensure neither of you pays for a crime you didn't commit. I can't make the charges or the warrants or the manhunt go away, but I can make *you* go away. That one-way trip, loaded with dough, to a beautiful, balmy country with no U.S. extradition treaty might not have been such a bogus idea. I'm a guy who can make it happen just like that." He snapped his fingers.

Maddie gasped, and Chris opened his mouth to speak, but David raised a forestalling hand.

"Don't answer me now. Sleep on it. Give yourselves one more night to decide your future." Their host rose and silently departed the room.

Chris stared at Maddie, and Maddie stared back at him.

"That was... Wow!" she said.

"We couldn't possibly."

"No, of course not. That option is against everything we set out to do."

"Absolutely."

Their words were definite, but the tone of each bold remark was not. Was the temptation as real to her as it was to him?

Maddie rubbed her palms against her jeans. "Then I guess there's nothing to say. We'll give David our answer in the morning."

"David?"

"Is there any other filthy rich guy in this house who offered to fund our early retirement at a tropical resort?"

"No, I was just surprised. This is the first time you've called my friend by his first name."

"I suppose that's true." Her gaze dropped. "I like him. *This* David. I'm sure I would have despised the person he was before Christ did in him only what He can do. I don't know if David committed the crime the evidence suggests. He doesn't, either. But the man he's become is worth knowing."

"I agree."

"Maybe that's why we're both secretly considering taking him up on his offer."

Chris let out a brief chuckle through is nose. "We're a pair, all right."

"I think so."

She gave him a look that thrilled him to the soles of his feet. This special thing coming to fruition between them was another huge nudge toward David's solution. If justice was to be denied them, why shouldn't they grab a little happiness instead? Why should they risk their freedom and their potential love on an insane gamble?

"Chris?"

He looked up to realize Maddie stood sideways in the doorway, gazing at him with eyes that shimmered.

"I'm not done crying," she said.

Chris nodded and patted the still-damp shoulder of his shirt.

She ghosted a smile and then was gone.

That did it. Maddie deserved every chance he could give her to soak his shoulder with her tears. She deserved peace and safety, not another reason to sob and no shoulder to wet because they were torn apart by a justice system gone awry.

FIFTEEN

The hours of the night held little sleep for Maddie. She flopped over and over until her covers wrapped her like a mummy. Finally, she fought free of the sheet and blanket and rose to prowl her end of the house. Each window she passed revealed an ebony sky lit by a full, golden moon and attended by glittering stars, but the clear night didn't help clarify her thoughts.

She loved Chris. It was too soon to tell him so, but a guarded hope accompanied that realization. Guarded because stubborn insistence on their current course was all too likely to end with them in prison or worse. If it was only herself to consider, she'd say risk it all, but the mental image of Chris sentenced to live the remainder of his life behind bars or condemned to lethal injection for the murder of a DEA agent turned her stomach inside out. For him, she couldn't risk that outcome. Flight rather than fight went against every ounce of instinct and training within her, but for him she'd behave counterintuitively.

In the wee hours, decision made, she burrowed into her bed covers and entered exhausted, fitful sleep.

The sound of male voices and scents of cooking food from the kitchen awakened her. She checked the bedside clock and sighed. She'd slept half the morning away, but felt anything but refreshed.

Groaning, Maddie piled out of bed and threw on some clothes, then made herself presentable with a brush through her hair and a brush on her teeth. Soldiers were trained to perform the necessaries in near light speed, so she joined the guys for breakfast in the kitchen within five minutes of rising.

Chris stood at the stove, cooking eggs and bacon, while David minded the toaster and poured orange juice into glasses at the counter next to the refrigerator. As she padded toward them in stocking feet, the men halted their small talk about a fascinating topic—the weather—and turned their heads toward her. She awarded them both a smile, but sought to engage Chris's gaze with hers. He met her look steady-on, and her eyes widened. He'd made his decision also. Could she hope that they were on the same page about what must be done?

"Hey, there. Hope you slept well." Chris smiled, but his gaze searched hers. Dark circles under his eyes announced that his night of rest had been as short as hers. "How do you like your eggs?"

"Any way you fix them." She wandered to the center island and settled onto a stool. "If I'm not cooking, I'm not fussy."

"Allow us to serve you." David set a glass of orange juice on the counter in front of her.

"Lovely idea." She lifted the glass to her lips.

In short order, the men had steaming plates prepared. Chris crutched over to the stool beside her. He gave her shoulder a squeeze as he sat down, and she offered a smile that was tentative at best. Too much lay undecided between them. David delivered a heartfelt blessing over the food, and then they all tucked in with varying degrees of gusto.

Her enthusiasm for food was unfortunately poor, but she made herself swallow, bite by bite, what normally she would have gobbled. Her appetite had fallen prey to nerves about what the post-breakfast discussion might hold. At last, they shoved their plates away and leaned back in their chairs. Sipping at the last of her juice, she looked from one man to the other. David's expression was suspiciously bland. Chris's face betrayed tension in the deepened crows'-feet at the edges of his eyes.

"What are you waiting for, Mason?" She set her empty glass on the table. "The next solar eclipse? I'd like to hear your decision."

David chuckled. "Direct, isn't she?"

"No bushes get beaten on her watch," Chris answered.

"Har-de-har." Maddie fought a chuckle. Levity was not the order of the hour. "I'm all ears."

"Ladies first."

"You *would* pull that one on me." She wrinkled her nose. "Very well." Her gaze found David's. "How soon can you get us out of here?"

Their host's sharp stare traveled to Chris. "Now you."

"Yeah, what she said." His chin firmed, and he jerked a nod.

David slapped a palm to the table. "Looks like I have some phone calls to make from my office. Enjoy transferring these dishes to the dishwasher." He got up.

"No problem." Maddie rose.

Chris reached for his crutches, but she snatched them and moved them out of reach.

"No fair!" He subsided onto his stool.

"Totally fair. You cooked. I'll clean up. Besides, I'm not going to have you fall over while you try to carry dishes and handle crutches at the same time."

David exited the room, snickering.

Maddie busied herself with filling the dishwasher. Silence fell. The quiet should have felt peaceful. After all, they'd made their decisions, and the choices had matched. Instead, Maddie's stomach tensed by micrometers with every passing moment. She kept her gaze to herself. No need to display her unease, particularly when she couldn't explain it, even to herself.

A small *scritch-scratch* sound drew a sidelong look toward Chris. He was staring at his walking boot, propped up on a chair, and pulling the Velcro loose then refastening it, over and over. He looked as unhappy as she felt.

"I'm relieved you're not going to run the risk of landing in prison," he said. "I couldn't stand that."

Maddie slapped the dishwasher door closed. "I don't care about myself. If I thought you'd let me stay behind to finish this and let the chips fall where they may, I'd wave to your jet fumes in a heartbeat. But I figure you're too stubborn for that."

"Me!" Chris snorted. "You give new depth of meaning to the word. I knew you'd never leave the country without me, and somebody has got to look out for you."

Maddie's face heated. "What do you mean by that remark, Mason? You've appointed yourself as my protector? You forget which one of us is the bodyguard."

Chris's cheeks burst red. "You need someone to protect you from yourself, Ms. Ranger, and I'd make any sacrifice to see to your safety."

"Sacrifice! That's what you think about going away with me?"

Choking on words, Maddie whirled and leaned on the counter with both hands. More of those dratted tears threatened. She was taking what Chris said the wrong way, but this whole direction felt like a wrong turn.

A warm hand fell on her shoulder. Maddie turned and let herself become wrapped Chris's offered embrace.

"I'm sorry." Her voice came out muffled against his

shoulder. "I thought I could do this. I want to…for you." The waterworks kicked in over her best efforts to stop them, and sobs shook her shoulders. "I feel like…a failure. Can't even do…the sensible thing…for you."

"You beautiful, wonderful, crazy woman." Chris's voice oozed tenderness. "Guess that makes us a pair of crazies, because I can't run, either."

Maddie sniffed long and hard then looked up into his eyes. "We'd hate each other eventually."

"I don't know if I could ever hate you, but I think we're agreed that we have to go for it, come flash flood or hot place?"

"Yep." She straightened her spine, swiped the tears from her face, and backed away. "The ranger creed is too much a part of me. Our vows say straight out that *surrender* is not a ranger word." She drew herself to attention. "'Readily will I display the intestinal fortitude required to fight on to the ranger objective and complete the mission though I be the lone survivor.'"

Chris's fingertips traced a burning path around her cheekbone to the tip of her chin. "You're not alone. We're going to stick together through this. And if it turns out well, then maybe…" His Adam's apple bobbed, and he seemed about to say something, but he cleared his throat and dropped his gaze.

Maybe what? Was she ready for him to make some kind of love commitment? Probably not. Still, she swallowed disappointment at his nondeclaration. At least she had someone steady and strong beside her for this last leg of the mission, just like he'd been a rock throughout.

"I've felt alone so often over the past year, but no more. In you, I see that the civilian soul can burn with the credo of no give-up and no compromise."

"So I'm an honorary ranger?"

"Better than that. You're a man of honor, no matter what vocation or situation you're in."

"Thanks. It means a lot to me that you would say that." His voice cracked at the end of the sentence.

Maddie let out a watery laugh. "Don't *you* go all teary on *me*. We'll flood David out of his house."

Gazing into each other's faces, they shared a long chuckle.

"We'd better tell David to call off his evacuation plans on our behalf," Chris said.

"Right. The poor guy seemed so excited he could do such a big thing for us."

Maddie helped Chris collect his crutches, and they headed up the hallway toward the study. Her feet could have been treading on a pillow as light as her spirits had become. Totally irrational with the weight of storm clouds hanging over their heads, but she was starting to learn not to question the moment.

They found David with his feet up on his desk, pecking away at his smart phone.

"Hey, buddy," Chris said when he looked up. "We will never be able to repay you for all you've done, but it looks like you'll have to put those great escape plans aside. Maddie and I have decided to charge the dragon, swords swinging."

David stared at them, thumbs poised over his phone screen.

Maddie chuckled. "What this word-meister is trying to say is that we're going to finish the mission."

Chris sent her a raised-brow look. "What the warrior princess is trying to say—"

"I know what you're both saying." David grinned and plopped his feet to the floor. "I was just playing a little Angry Birds."

"A video game?"

"Nothing else to do." He shrugged. "I figured if I gave you two a little alone time, you'd figure out what you really wanted to do."

Maddie scowled. "You weren't serious about setting us up outside the U.S.?"

"A hundred and ten percent. You could already be on my private jet, but I couldn't wrap my head around either one of you tucking tail." He rubbed his hands together. "Now, how can I aide the cause of justice?"

She looked at Chris. "Here's the go-to guy for a fresh plan."

Chris tapped the end of his chin. "I've been toying with a couple of thoughts. It really depends on who we choose to trust with the evidence."

"And your best investigative-reporter hunch is?"

"You're not going to like it."

"You've proposed a lot of ideas I haven't liked, but they've all worked out better than I thought they would. Spill, Mason."

He told her, and he was right. She didn't like it.

The brick high-rise speared the night sky over San Antonio. Only scattered windows glowed with light. Gazing up at the tower from the back of David's limousine, Chris bit the inside of his lip. His inference about FBI Special Agent Blunt's whereabouts had better be accurate. News reports hadn't come right out and said so, but the wording hinted that since he and Maddie had dropped off the radar, the lead agent in the investigation had returned to his home base at the San Antonio Field Office. But by eleven on any ordinary night, he should be relaxing at home.

Maybe. If a lot of factors were just right—such as no

other emergencies driving him to burn the midnight oil at the office.

Chris gnawed his lip harder. Maddie trusted him now, and he couldn't afford to blow that precious commodity. If only at this moment, his idea didn't seem so hare-brained. Good thing his expression wasn't clear to the other passengers in the dimness. The sight wouldn't inspire confidence. What if he was wrong? What if this guy's shoes-too-tight personality didn't indicate a straight-and-narrow character?

"Are you sure you want to do this, David?" he asked the shadowed figure in the driver's seat. "Involving yourself directly could get you in major trouble."

David lifted a dismissive hand. "Been there, done that, got the T-shirt. I intend to enjoy this."

Chris blew air through his teeth in a low whistle. "All right then. Let's get this show on the road."

Next to him, Maddie chuckled. "Correction. We've been on the road for hours and hours. Now it's time to get on our feet and go after the objective."

"That's my cue," David said and opened his car door.

Not waiting for the chauffeur act, Maddie climbed out and turned to help Chris with his crutches. David met them on the sidewalk and then led the way to the building's intercom board. He stood where the security camera could get a good look at him. Maddie and Chris stayed out of sight to the side.

"Apartment 819," Chris said.

"Check." David pressed the buzzer button.

Shortly—too fast for the man to have been asleep—a gruff voice demanded to know who was outside.

"David Greene."

The silence lasted long enough to betray the agent's

surprise. "David Greene, as in the Alicia Gonzales murder case David Greene?"

"In the flesh."

"What brings you to my door?"

"I have to confess."

Again the telling pause. "Listen, Greene, if this is some kind of rich-boy joke, or you're too wasted for common sense just climb back onto your flying carpet and sail out of here. I've got no time to waste on a lost cause."

"No joke, and I'm more sober than the judge who presided at my Grand Jury hearing."

"What are you doing at my door? The case belongs to the local PD."

"Let's just say I want a pair of fresh ears to hear what I have to say."

The intercom stayed silent for several heartbeats. Chris's mouth went dry.

"All right, you've got my attention," Blunt said. "Why don't I meet you at the office in an hour? We'll roll out the red carpet."

"We talk right here, right now, with you alone, or not ever."

Another pause dragged on until sweat popped out on Chris's forehead. So much had to go right for this plan to work.

"Come in," Blunt said, and the front door buzzed.

David pulled the door open wide and went through. Then he waited a few seconds, long enough for Blunt to have lost interest in watching his security screen. Then he turned to let Maddie and Chris in. They proceeded through an empty lobby directly to the elevator.

"Anyone need a refresher on the procedure?" Maddie asked on the way to the eighth floor.

"I'm good," David said.

"Me, too," Chris confirmed.

"Good men." Maddie's grin contained a bit of the shark.

Chris suppressed a shiver. *Watch out, Mr. Shoes-Too-Tight Agent.*

The elevator door *dinged* open, and David got out first, followed by Maddie—a swift and silent shadow. Chris tagged along slowly enough that the distinctive sound of his crutches would not carry to the agent through his door. Ahead, David reached the apartment, but stopped and waited while Maddie took up a position against the wall nearest the door knob. She gave him a nod, and David knocked.

On the other side of the door, a chain rattled. Chris was close enough to hear the sound, but lagging too far behind to see the action firsthand. The door swung open and Maddie lunged inside. A loud grunt, a thud and a curse in a masculine tone carried to him.

Chris put some hustle in his crutching and reached the doorway half out of breath. David admitted him, and Chris swung over the threshold to find a lanky man facedown on the entry hall carpet with Maddie's knee in the small of his back and his right hand twisted up between his shoulder blades. A gun lay farther up the hallway where it must have been knocked away. Clearly, the very special Agent Blunt was not a trusting man—even when he thought he had a willing confessor on his doorstep.

"Agent Blunt," David said, "I'm here to confess that Christopher Mason is my friend. As far as whether or not *I* ever did anything worthy of the charge of murder, I don't know for sure, but I do know that Chris didn't kill anyone, and he's certainly not in cahoots with a drug cartel. However, he does have knowledge that should be of interest to you. I think you should listen to what he has to say."

"Absolutely," the man on the floor gasped out. "Get

this she-tiger off me, and we'll talk. We're eager to know what you've got."

"We?" Chris crutched closer, but Maddie sent him a glare that halted his approach. He trusted her control of the situation and backed off.

"Yes." Agent Blunt lifted his head and rippled his body, as if to work free of the hold on him. Maddie shifted more weight onto her knee, and he subsided with a groan.

"Go ahead and talk," Maddie said. "Just don't try to move."

Blunt gusted out a breath. "I'm part of a select internal task force composed of members known only to each other and the director. We know there's someone dirty in-house. We're also reasonably certain that you didn't kill DEA Agent Edgar Jackson."

"Then why the manhunt for us?" Chris demanded.

"It would have tipped our hand to whoever is dirty, not just in our agency but others, if we questioned their story about having an eyewitness identify you two at the scene of the crime."

Chris locked gazes with Maddie. He couldn't answer the question on her face. Was Blunt toying with them, trying to trip them up, or was he serious?

"But we *were* at the scene of the crime," he told the agent. A fresh stillness gripped the man's body. "We were too late to speak to a living Edgar Jackson, but we'd just missed the killer—someone who knew our next stop was likely to be Jackson's house."

"Do you know who that someone is?"

"Pretty sure. We've got a fascinating voice recording and a riveting video from a little operation we ran at a hotel in downtown Laredo. We also had a pretty entertaining run-in with some surprising folks the day before the hotel caper, but a bullet ripped my recorder out of my hand. Maddie and I heard enough of the conversation to give you what we believe to be the date, time and place of the next shipment across the border. How interested are you in all this?"

"Very." Blunt nodded. "The director will authorize protective custody and immunity from prosecution for yourselves and anyone who helped you, as long as your information is accurate and leads to the apprehension of the conspirators operating within the United States."

"Our information is accurate, but whether or not it leads to the apprehension of the guilty parties is up to your people."

"That's the deal. Are *you* interested?"

Chris looked at David, who jerked his chin in the affirmative.

Chris frowned. His friend might be too quick to trust. Law enforcement was rabid to pin anything on David Greene. "Does that offer of immunity extend to David here?"

A pregnant pause followed. Finally, Blunt huffed. "Only as far as aiding and abetting you two. Any other charge is still fair game."

"Agreed," David said.

Chris nodded to Maddie. She hopped up and backed away from the agent, but appropriated the man's gun in the process. Watchful woman.

Agent Blunt got up slowly, rubbing his arm and shoulder. "Ms. Jerrard, you could give lessons in hand-to-hand to our FBI trainers." He turned and led the way into a living room furnished in crisp sterility.

The guy actually did walk like his shoes were too tight—only he wasn't wearing anything but socks on his feet. Chris shared a small smile with Maddie. She knew exactly what he was thinking. Crazy wonderful how their minds were in sync.

The agent faced them, arms crossed, gaze stern. "It might increase your trust factor to know that I'm the person who made sure the heat lifted sufficiently for you to pop your heads aboveground. It didn't take much more than a mention within a reporter's earshot that you two might already have skipped the country, and the idea made the news."

"I knew that wasn't natural," Maddie said. "But it never occurred to me that the report was part of a plan to help us."

"It has always been the plan to catch whoever masterminded the Rio Grande Massacre. Helping you is secondary."

"Peripheral might be more like it." Maddie poked the air with her forefinger. "Your investigation concluded our ranger scout was to blame. You don't care who you hurt unjustly."

"Our report merely *suggested* carelessness of the scout as a possible scenario. Again, the media pounced on an aspect that offered a ready explanation to the public."

Chris snorted. "Don't blame the media for your deliberate misdirection of the American people." No wonder Maddie couldn't stand this guy.

"Regardless of whether you approve of our methods, we do get the job done, and at the moment, our goals are mutually compatible." A feral gleam entered the man's eyes. "Show me what you've got."

SIXTEEN

A lonesome wind—bitter with the tang of sand, mesquite and chola—moaned faintly through the maze of draws and washes in this lonely stretch along the Texas side of the Rio Grande River. Representative Jess's land.

It was the Fourth of July at 11:55 p.m. Maddie waited beside Chris in an open-air, two-seater ATV a little back from the mixed band of DEA and FBI personnel lying in wait for whatever might occur in the next few minutes.

If anything.

She glanced at Chris's profile outlined in the shimmer of light from a three-quarter moon. He stared stoically ahead. She turned her face forward as well, ears straining for the jingle of a bridle bit or the hum of ATVs similar to their own transportation or the *swish-swish* of oars from boats—anything to indicate the approach of smugglers. Nothing but that lonesome wail and the rustle of flowing water. Her stomach roiled.

What if they were wrong? Maybe they'd misinterpreted what they heard at that meeting in the paper mill. A lot was riding on them being right. Not least of which was the immunity deal for themselves plus David and even Bonita, if her assistance to wanted fugitives ever became known. Not that Maddie and Chris would ever tell. Without solid results from this bust, she had no doubt the feds would find something to pin on them, maybe even that murder charge Blunt had tried to tell them was bogus. Unfortunately, there was enough circumstantial evidence to make a case if an ambitious D.A. wanted to take it on.

Maybe Jess and his bunch had rescheduled the shipment. Had they grown paranoid of their plans despite the care taken to alleviate their concerns? Attention to Agent Jackson's murder investigation and the disappearance of the main suspects had died down in the media. Blunt said the case was still open on agents' desks but pretty much considered cold until the next lead came as to Chris's and her whereabouts. Surely, all of these factors would have reassured Jess and his right-hand man, Richard Glick— that disgrace to a ranger uniform.

During their enforced hiding in a safe house that was nothing like David Greene's lovely home, Blunt had accommodated them with information about Glick. The man had achieved the rank of sergeant, but resigned in a deal to forestall charges of unusual cruelty to new recruits. Considering the grueling nature of ranger training, the issue must have been pretty severe. Glick had been a bad apple within the army, and he was worse outside of the uniform.

Chris hissed in a breath, and Maddie hauled her mind back into the moment. When she was on active duty, she would never have been so easily distracted. Was she growing more civilian? She couldn't afford to relax that much until she took down Jess, and Glick, and all who cost her comrades in arms their lives.

Sure enough, Chris had heard what she'd been slow to pick out—the soft *clip-clop* of hooves, approaching from the U.S. side. And then there came the other half expected, half-hoped-for sound, the *shush* of oars moving in from the Mexico side. The shipment was on!

Maddie's heart rate spurred into a gallop. Chris gripped her hand and squeezed.

Minutes trickled past. One minute. Two. Five minutes. Eight. Ten minutes. The sound but not the sense of voices drifted to them—some Hispanic-accented, others American. Someone among them barked a laugh.

Then a spotlight suddenly glared. Maddie winced at the brilliance, but gnashed her teeth that she could not see what it illuminated. Agent Blunt's voice rang out, commanding the smugglers to instant surrender. Pandemonium erupted, shouts and gunshots and running feet, but she and Chris were situated in such a place they couldn't see anything that was happening. They were too far away and on the other side of a hump of ground.

Unacceptable.

"I'm going in," she told Chris.

He gripped her hand tighter. "We were ordered to stay out of this. It was amazing they granted our presence at all. Besides, how are you going to get past our watchdog driver in the seat ahead of us?"

"He's fully engaged in what's happening ahead. He won't even notice when I slip away."

"Don't count on it."

"Trust me." She disengaged her hand from his.

"I don't like it."

A fresh spate of gunfire and shouts rang out, and Chris leaned forward. Maddie slid from the seat of the ATV. His voice followed her, still talking as if she was there beside him. The driver's head didn't so much as turn as she melted into the night.

Faint trails of moonlit phosphorescence in the sand guided her feet. She climbed a gentle rise. At the top she found a perch that let her see the action illuminated by the spotlight. She hunkered down onto her belly and took in the scene.

Little pockets of smugglers were already rounded up and being herded away. She didn't see Glick among them. Disappointing. They had expected he would be the man on the ground for Representative Jess. The sound and flash of gunfire in one of the draws betrayed at least one pocket of resistance. Maybe he was pinned down there.

A flicker of movement in the shadows to her right caught Maddie's attention. She focused on the spot and little by little made out the form of a large man moving with the fluid grace of a puma. He was slinking away from the conflict. Glick?

Thank you, God, for this opportunity to deal with a snake.

She'd give a lot for a sidearm right now, but gun or no gun, she was going to stop this reptile. He had to pay. She moved from her hillock and began to imitate the movement of the enemy on a trajectory to intercept. He seemed to be heading for a small cut in the earth about twenty yards distant. If she cried out she would alert him that his escape was noticed, and he could disappear in any of a dozen directions. No, she needed to maintain stealth and keep her eyes upon him.

Maddie risked quickening her pace. She climbed upward, aiming for the lip of the wash. If she was to have any chance against an armed man, she needed to drop down on him unexpectedly from above. She reached the top edge of the slit in the ground as her quarry entered the cut. His head was only a few feet below her. There wouldn't be a better moment. She launched herself downward and struck a human tank.

Her attack startled a yelp and a stagger from him, but he threw her off as if she were a rabbit pouncing on a panther.

She hit the ground, rolled and came up, foot swinging for the gleam that was her adversary's gun. The pistol flew and hit the wall of the wash with a dull clatter.

Cursing, the man whirled and struck out at her with a giant paw. The wind of his swing fanned her face as she lurched backward, more from poor footing than intentional avoidance. If he'd connected, she'd already be down for the count. Engaging this sort of enemy in close quarters was a bad move. At least it would be, if she were truly alone. Now that he was aware of her presence, she had nothing to lose by calling for help.

Maddie opened her mouth to let out a scream, but a kick to her solar plexus landed her breathless on her back, pain screeching through her body. Her adversary's foot had landed only a glancing blow, yet she was immobilized and speechless. If the hit had landed as intended, it could have killed her. Struggling for air, mind hazy with pain, she gazed up at the moon, and then a face hove into view. A face she knew.

The familiar dread swallowed her mind, but this was no nightmare of memory. This was real. This was now. And Glick had recovered his gun. He pointed it down at her, thick lips drawn back in a sneer. A fresh spate of gunfire erupted from a draw many yards away. He smiled.

"No one will hear and come running," he said. "This time I'm going to take the shot."

The muzzle flashed even as a rush of movement turned his head. Fresh pain seared through Maddie, spreading flaming tentacles through her chest, but she didn't miss a moment as a thick branch of driftwood slashed out of the dark and thudded into Glick's head. The man dropped like a stone.

That's all she needed to see. Satisfaction flooded in as consciousness winked out.

* * *

Chris gaped in horror at the wetness spreading across Maddie's chest. He fell to his knees and pressed his hands over the hemorrhage even as he cried out for help.

"Don't you dare leave me," he barked to her limp form, then hollered again for someone—anyone—to bring the paramedics. He leaned down close toward her ear. "Hear me, woman! I love you, and I'm not going to lose you now!"

The crunch of multiple feet running in the sand brought his head up. Within minutes, the paramedics that had been standing by were swarming over Maddie. He stood helplessly to the side, fists clenching and unclenching, as they labored over her. Then they loaded her on a stretcher and headed away. Shrugging off restraining hands, whose they were he didn't know or care, he hobbled after the medical personnel.

His ankle had improved dramatically between this night and when he'd injured it, but it still slowed him too much to keep up with the paramedics' brisk pace. Thank God, he hadn't allowed the weakness and twinges of discomfort to prevent him from following Maddie and decking Glick when he did. But had he been quick enough?

The last words Chris overheard before the paramedics outstripped him turned his legs to jelly and his heart to stone.

"...don't know if she'll make it..."

SEVENTEEN

An annoying, steady beep nagged Maddie to consciousness. The accompanying mix of biological and antiseptic smells betrayed her location. A hospital room.

So that dirty dog Glick didn't do her in after all. She hadn't expected to awaken on this planet, much less in full possession of her most recent memory—Chris wielding a big stick like a major league home-run hitter.

Chris!

Her heart rate jumped, and the timing of the beeps followed suit. Where was he? What happened after she passed out? Was Chris all right? She wrenched her eyes open. The lids parted with a sting as if they'd been glued together. How long had she been out of it?

"Hey, there! Take it easy, beautiful."

The scolding fondness of the words meant little compared to the treasure of hearing the voice that spoke them. A familiar face obstructed her view of the white ceiling.

"Chri-i-i-s." The word escaped her dry throat in a drawled croak.

"I'm here, darlin'. Never left your side."

A strong hand gripped one of hers and squeezed. His appearance testified to a vigil of some length. She'd never seen his famous face scruffy with unshaved whiskers, but he'd never looked more adorable. She could hardly talk with this bothersome tube down her throat, but maybe her eyes were telling him how she felt. His baby blues were a bit bloodshot and puffy, like someone sleep-deprived, but his grin beamed white and strong and did its usual number on her insides. The infernal beeping machine echoed the jig of her pulse.

"Thank God, you're on the mend. I almost lost you, and I couldn't bear the thought." The corners of Chris's eyes twitched and a suspicious sheen coated them. He took a quick swipe at his face without losing his grin. "I'll let someone know you're awake, and you'd probably like to be let loose of the wires and tubing."

Maddie answered with a vigorous nod. Chris backed away from the bed as if he couldn't take his gaze off her. Hers followed him—devoured him—until the door *shushed* closed behind him. He'd come to her rescue in the crucial instant when death would have taken her, then stayed by her side while she found her toehold on life again, but would they soon say goodbye and part ways?

She didn't want that—oh, how she didn't! But how did she halt the inevitable? The entire time they'd striven together for a single-minded goal of justice they'd told themselves and each other that there could be no future together. But why not? What kept them apart *now?*

Only the condition of their hearts. Or his, rather. She knew the condition of hers. She loved Christopher Mason— had done so for a lot longer than she'd been willing to admit. But did she dare hope his concern for her hinted that he returned the sentiment? Why would he want a stubborn, tough-girl like her when he could have—and surely deserved—any dainty, sophisticated beauty of his choice?

Her chest ached with far more than a healing bullet wound.

* * *

Chris settled Maddie in a chair in the small hospital solarium, then stood back and watched her tilt her face up to the sun's rays bathing her through the windows. It had been a full day since she awakened from her forty-eight-hour coma, and already she was restless and up walking around. However, the amount of weight she leaned on his arm during their jaunt up the hallway betrayed lingering weakness from loss of blood.

She'd been quiet—too quiet for his peace of mind. What was she thinking in that nimble brain of hers? More important, what did she feel for him? Gratitude, for sure. She'd made that abundantly clear, but he owed her just as much, if not more. He ground his teeth together. A friendly relationship based on mutual admiration was the last thing he wanted.

Chris hauled in a deep breath. What was that old saying? No guts, no glory? Well, he was about to put the theory to the ultimate test where his heart was concerned. Either he'd find hope of winning a prize worth far more than any sports trophy or spoils of war, or he would leave empty—but at least he'd know. This not knowing was driving him nuts.

Clearing his throat, Chris settled into a chair beside her, and her tawny gaze met his. Wariness crept into her expression. Chris hooded his gaze, and kneaded his knees with his hands. If he looked half as petrified as he felt, no wonder she was puzzled. But he hadn't made a declaration of this sort to any woman since Robin, and look how that had turned out. Not that he feared Maddie turning on him and shooting him. At least not literally.

"If you don't spit it out, Mason, you're going to bust. Don't treat me with kid gloves. What? Something went wrong with the bust, and the bad guys are going to get off?"

Chris chuckled. "That's the worst thing you can think of?"

"No, but it's pretty bad."

"Roger that, but there's every indication that the bad guys are in the bag to stay."

"Then what?" The vestige of color in her cheeks leaked away. "You're looking for a graceful way to say goodbye? Don't worry about it, Mason. I'll be fine."

Maddie turned her head away, but not before Chris glimpsed the tremble of her lips. The too-strong-for-her-own-good woman didn't want him to leave. His heart leaped.

She lifted a dismissive hand. "I know you've got important reporting business to take care of. I—"

"Will you hush long enough for me to keep a promise I made to myself and God while you lay hovering between here and heaven?"

"What promise was that?" Her head turned slightly toward him, though her gaze remained lowered and her fingers picked at the terry cloth of her robe. "Has to be pretty serious if it's a deathbed vow—even though it wasn't your deathbed."

Pulse throbbing in his temples, Chris lifted her chin and looked square into her shadowed gaze. "I promised that if only I had the chance to speak to you again, I would confess the truth, no matter the risk."

"The truth?" Her eyes widened and she pulled away. "You don't have to convince me about the Rio anymore, Chris. I know you didn't betray our forces, but maybe you think you made some kind of mistake that night—"

"The only mistake I made on the Rio is not stepping out of the shadows and kissing you like I longed to do. And I would make the mistake worse by not being honest with you now. I love you, Madeleine Jerrard. I love you with a ferocity that scares me silly. I think I've loved you for a long time, but was too bullheaded to face up to feelings I had convinced myself I shouldn't have."

An odd sound escaped the woman to whom he was confessing his love, something between a snort and a squeak, and her face puckered. A tear spilled out one eye.

Chris tentatively wiped wetness from her cheek with the ball of his forefinger. "Don't cry, sweetheart. I'm not making any demands. I don't even have any expectations—just a hope that you might be willing to go on seeing me. Or, more like, for me to go on seeing you. I—"

"Mason, you talk too much." She leaned toward him, and another tear escaped. "Never tell a woman not to cry when her dreams have just come true."

The breath hung up in Chris's throat. He swallowed. "Then there's a chance I could win your heart?"

She shook her head. "Too late. It's already long gone. You'll find it in your pocket."

His jaw gaped and then a laugh burst out. "I've been a bundle of nerves for nothing."

"Oh, I wouldn't say nothing." She poked a finger against his breastbone. "Just because I already love you doesn't mean I'm not going to make you court me."

"That's one challenge I plan to relish." Courting this fiery, headstrong woman would be the biggest headache, but the most fun he'd ever had.

He opened his arms, and she melted into them where she belonged. Their laughter mingled, and then their lips.

EIGHTEEN

Five Months Later

"You were delusional, Mason, if you thought a little bullet nick was going to keep me from marrying you."

Maddie would twirl on her tiptoes if her spike heels didn't already have her on her toes, and if they weren't standing in the midst of august company in an elegantly appointed anteroom of the state's capitol building. She smiled back at Chris's frown. He looked sensational in his tailored suit, and she hadn't minded her reflection in the mirror when she donned her flowing, emerald-colored formal in her hotel room. She could do without the height of these spike heels, but at least Chris was tall enough not to be topped by her added inches.

"And your delusions continue," he pronounced.

"Explain yourself, Mr. Investigative Reporter."

He wagged a forefinger in her direction. "Just because the bullet didn't hit any vital organs it does not qualify the wound as a nick. It was a through-and-through, but you're not ready to admit how close I came to losing you."

"Awww! Poor baby." She tugged on the lapel of his suit. "The bullet *nicked* an artery."

Chris sniffed. "A rather life-threatening detail, don't you think?"

"God was merciful."

"No argument there."

Maddie held her hand in front of her and admired the fat rock on her index finger. Chris had placed it there only last week over an intimate dinner in the private alcove of a fancy restaurant. He'd done his part by courting her like a princess, so she'd done her part by saying yes.

Chris linked his dark-suited arm with her silk-clad elbow. "Lovely," he said.

"The ring or me?" She arched a brow at him.

"Both, but you more so."

"Diplomatic response, but do you mean that or are you trying to get on my good side?"

"Again, both."

They grinned at each other.

Chris and she were waiting for their cue to step out and receive a public award given to very few civilians for extraordinary public service. They'd already been treated to a private banquet with the governor and senior aides and legislators, both state and federal. Soon they were to be introduced to a much larger body of dignitaries who'd enjoyed a banquet in the ballroom.

As weeks and months slid by, the fuse they helped ignite had exploded into a massive exposé of great and small cogs within multiple agencies and governmental bodies that fitted together in a network of conspirators all lining their pockets on the drug trade. In one swoop, a huge chunk had been torn from the hide of that hideous monster, which should take a fair amount of time to heal. She'd heard that law enforcement agencies across the country were hosting quiet internal celebrations in response.

Representative Jess and his strong-arm, Richard Glick, were among those undergoing indictment. Those two, as well as agents Ramsey and Lesko, among others, were being held without bail until their trials.

Results didn't get much better. So what if a smile the size of her home state seemed to have taken up permanent residence on her face? The expression belonged there. Not that there weren't loose ends to tie up—like who on the ground with her team the night of the massacre betrayed the location of their camp to the cartel? Every once in a while, she still lost sleep over that question. Maybe she wouldn't know the answer this side of eternity. With this wonderful man by her side, she'd do her best to come to terms with the missing puzzle piece.

"Pssst!" The hiss drew her head around to see Agent Blunt motioning for them to step into a connecting office.

Chris winked at her and tugged her toward the other room. What could be so important that they might miss their cue to step on stage? Not that she was all that eager for the spotlight, but a person didn't say no to the governor when he insisted on throwing a shindig. Chris and she stepped into the nicely decorated office, and Blunt shut the door. The agent led the way to a large chart laid out on a round table toward the right side of the room.

"I put the request through on your behalf, Mason, and got permission from the Director to show you this." He waved toward what turned out not to be a chart but a computer-generated map of an area along the Rio Grande.

Maddie's heartbeat stuttered. She recognized the spot all too well—the site of the massacre.

"As part of our investigation," the FBI agent continued, "we made this detailed representation of the location of every person, every dead body and every piece of equipment or property recovered from the scene."

Chris grabbed Maddie's hand and squeezed. Her heart

began to beat normally again, though her lungs struggled to pull in a full breath.

"Point out where my fiancée was found," Chris said.

"Right here." Blunt placed a fingertip on a dot labeled: *Jerrard—recovered alive—shrapnel wound to the head— broken bones.*

Chris turned toward her, gaze shadowed. "I've wanted to tell you about this, but for a long time I knew you wouldn't believe me. Then these past months I didn't want to interrupt our happiness by belaboring dark history."

Maddie's insides tensed. What bombshell was about to drop now? "Go on."

"After I carried you clear of the camp where shells were falling like rain, someone opened fire on us with a gun. We nearly bought it more than once. Finally, I took cover behind a clump of rocks. Then you regained consciousness long enough to draw your sidearm and return fire."

She rocked back on her heels. What an act not to remember! And where was this topic headed?

"I requested that the FBI allow us to see this map," Chris went on, "so that maybe, just maybe, we could determine who might have been taking potshots at us."

"One of the cartel forces, of course."

Chris shook his head. "Not necessarily."

"What are you getting at?"

"Look." He placed his finger on the spot labeled with her name then traced a line a few yards east. "This is the direction from which the bullets came."

The dot lay outside the encampment, but the name was familiar: *Hitchins—deceased—bullet wound to the chest.* Realization smacked Maddie in the face, along with an equal measure of denial.

"No." She shook her head. "I liked DEA Agent Lorraine Hitchins. She was my tent—" Air hissed between her teeth, and denial fled. "She was my tent mate—therefore, she had access to my communications equipment."

"Exactly." Blunt nodded his head. "I believe our agency will officially conclude that DEA Agent Hitchins was the leak that exposed your bivouac site to the cartel, and that you, army ranger Madeleine Jerrard, fired upon and killed Hitchins in self-defense."

Maddie gaped. "You mean the traitor of the Rio Grande Massacre has been dead all this time? And at my hand?"

Her mind reeled. She'd ached for justice to be served on the turncoat, and if truth be admitted, she'd wished on that person a large slice of vengeance served steaming hot. Never in her wildest dreams had she guessed the matter was already accomplished…or her role in it.

She looked up at Chris. "But my sidearm was missing when they picked me up out of the desert. I was told so and grilled about the missing piece over and over. I never could explain the issue to anyone's satisfaction—least of all to myself."

The FBI agent cleared his throat. "This is unofficial, and don't say you heard it from me, or I'll call you a liar." He shifted from one foot to another as if his shoes had shrunk another size. "Glick was on the ground with cartel forces that night and has admitted that he picked up your pistol when he happened upon you during his flight from incoming rescuers. He'd intended to shoot you with your own weapon, but absconded with it instead when he heard our people closing in."

Maddie's thoughts scurried like a hamster on a flywheel. She was beyond speech. This information explained so much.

"Are you implying that Glick is cooperating in the investigation?" Chris asked.

"You'd be amazed at what the difference between life

without possibility of parole compared to an assured sentence of lethal injection can wring out of a man's mouth—even one like Glick." A grin stretched Blunt's meager lips. "Tonight you're going to hear a special announcement from the governor related to this unadmitted cooperation, but I'm not letting that possum out of the sack one second early. Not if I want to keep my job."

The door opened behind them, and they turned as one. "Ms. Jerrard and Mr. Mason, they are ready for you," an aide announced in stodgy tones.

"Gotta go." Chris grabbed Maddie's hand and brought her knuckles to his lips.

The touch feathered reassurance into her soul. In a semi-haze, she allowed him to draw her onto the stage. A roar of applause greeted their appearance. The grand ballroom was full of people delivering a standing ovation from their banquet tables. Among the people were Bonita and David, and even Chris's sister, Serena, clapping and grinning beside a table near the stage.

Bonita looked elegant and happy in a fine gown no doubt purchased with the proceeds rolling in from her brother's book that Chris had begun to promote. Chris said the memoir was actually quite a powerhouse, and those who bought it seemed to agree. Since she couldn't rise to her feet, the older woman held up a pair of enthusiastic thumbs in between spates of applause.

Maddie offered Bonita a private smile, then jerked her thoughts into sharp focus and stood tall, chin high, surveying the crowd. This moment of honor was not for her. It was for her unrighteously slain comrades in arms. Only for them would she deliver a public speech, and only because Chris was beside her did her knees not knock audibly. After receiving her award from the governor's hands, she kept her acceptance speech blessedly brief and then let Chris do the rest of the talking for them. He could say what she felt much more eloquently anyway. After he concluded to riotous applause, she and Chris were ushered to privileged places at a table, front and center.

The governor took the podium, and a hush fell. The sixtysomething man surveyed the room gravely, then his sober face abruptly transformed into a mask of glee. He joined his hands above his head in a universal sign of victory. A ripple of speculation passed through the crowd, but the room fell silent as the governor, still smiling, cleared his throat into the microphone.

"As a direct result of intelligence gathered from drug smugglers captured during the daring ambush on the U.S. side of the Rio Grande five months ago, it is my privilege to announce that this very day a team of DEA Agents, army rangers and Mexican Federales stormed the hidden bastion of the Ortiz Drug Cartel. The stronghold was virtually annihilated, and every known leader of the cartel, including Fernando Ortiz himself, was either captured or eliminated."

The news struck Maddie like a bittersweet bludgeon. This should have been the announcement shared with the world after she and her unit took the cartel stronghold. But at least—at last—it had happened.

While the rest of the room erupted into applause and Texas hoorahs, she rose and lifted a hand to her forehead in salute to the American and Texas flags standing on the stage behind the governor. Beside her, Chris joined her in the silent tribute. Pressure built behind her forehead and cheekbones, and the backs of her eyes stung. She blinked against budding moisture and swallowed the thick golf ball gathering beneath her breastbone.

As the wild cheering continued, Chris leaned close to her ear. "Are you going to cry?"

"Later," she muttered out of the corner of her mouth.

"I look forward to the event." He smiled.

Smug man. He'd do well to remember that a wedding was pending. Then she'd have an entire lifetime to whip him into shape…or vice-versa. A rush of joy pushed the flood over the dam, and tears spilled down her cheeks.

Chuckling, Chris gathered her to himself and kissed her in front of God and country. Maddie kissed him back.

* * * * *

Dear Reader,

I'm delighted you joined me for Maddie and Chris's adventure. They went through quite a time of trial, didn't they? Not many of us will have to run and fight for our lives against ruthless foes determined to snuff out our lives. Aren't you glad? But we all experience trials and challenges that are just as dire and urgent to us. Nor do many of us experience such a public victory over evil, but our personal victories are just as important in the Kingdom of God.

My husband and I know a dear family of missionaries who at one time lived and worked in Nuevo Laredo, Mexico—sister city to Laredo, Texas. However, because of the rampant drug trade, Nuevo Laredo became so bloody and dangerous—even for innocent citizens—that they have moved their base of operations into the United States. Yet they continue to risk their lives by traveling back and forth between Mexico and the U.S. They do this for the love of God in order to reach men, women and particularly children with the Gospel and physical aid in the form of food, clothing and household items. Their journeys over the border are like traveling into a war zone.

It is vital to the missionaries' continued efforts that border agents wage an effective war against the rabid darkness that would like to flood our nation with poison. Therefore, I urge us all to "take up arms" in prayer to protect the lives of those who serve on the front lines of this war and to prosper their just cause. We have more power in the area of prayer than we think or that we use.

Feel free to check out my other books with Love Inspired Suspense. This is my sixth release with them. More information can be found on my website at:

http://www.jillelizabethnelson.com.

Every page of my website offers an opportunity to sign up for my quarterly enewsletter. Each issue contains encouraging words for life, breaking news in my writing life, and exclusive opportunities to win my books. You may also connect with me on Facebook at:

https://www.facebook.com/JillElizabethNelson.Author

Or on Twitter:

@ JillElizNelson.

Abundant blessings,
Jill E. Nelson
Endless Adventure~Timeless Truth
http://www.jillelizabethnelson.com

Questions for Discussion

1. Throughout much of the story, Maddie presumes Chris's guilt as the traitor who gave the cartel the location of their camp. She bases this assumption on the fact that he is the sole unscathed survivor of the massacre. Does this conclusion appear logical? Why or why not? Have you ever drawn a conclusion about a person or situation based on evidence that seemed conclusive to you, but later you discovered the truth to be quite different than what you assumed?

2. Chris resists his attraction to Maddie based on a personal philosophy adopted as a result of a tragic event early in his career. Does this personal philosophy proceed from logic or an instinct to protect himself (and others) from a repetition of his bad judgment? Have you ever created a personal rule of thumb or made an inner vow regarding future behavior? What was the root cause for this self-imposed regulation, and is this reason valid and valuable in your life? Why or why not?

3. Maddie's 1972 Oldsmobile Cutlass is precious to her. Why? Do you have an object in your life that is dear to you for a sentimental reason? What is the reason? What might be important enough to you to override the sentimental attachment and cause you to part with or destroy the item?

4. Maddie feels alone and abandoned—even by God. As much as she craves human and divine fellowship, she fears taking the risk of opening her heart. Is this

an understandable reaction, considering all she's been through? Why or why not? Discuss reasons why people close their hearts. Is your heart closed in any area? If so, why, and what would it take to heal that area and reopen your heart?

5. At the beginning of the story, Chris feels compelled to find Maddie and pursue the truth of what occurred that night in the Mexican desert. Why? Are his reasons principally personal or altruistic? What does Maddie think his reasons are? Why would she feel the need to put the worst possible construction on his motives?

6. How does Maddie deal with her grief over all the losses that have occurred in her life? Do you know people who are dealing with grief in a similar fashion? Are you among them? How does Scripture address the subject of grief, and how are these truths relevant to our lives? Is her progression from the beginning of the story, when she gives herself no time to cry, to the end of the story, when tears come freely, a healthy one? When are tears healthy and when are they not?

7. Maddie has a highly developed sense of justice. Chris has a highly developed nose for the truth. How do these individual characteristics create compatibility between them? How do they create clashes and misunderstandings?

8. Discuss the nontraditional roles of the main characters, with Maddie as the warrior/bodyguard and Chris as the intuitive thinker/planner. Do these dynamics work for the characters? If so, in what ways and why?

Does Scripture provide examples and provision for people who are called of God to fulfill roles in ways that may be nontraditional or countercultural? How do we sometimes limit ourselves and others by confining our thinking and expectations to our culture and traditions?

9. In spite of Maddie's nontraditional role and occupation, in what ways does she demonstrate her femininity, internally and externally? Despite Chris's dependency on Maddie for physical protection, in what ways does he demonstrate his masculinity, internally and externally?

10. Maddie and Chris realize their love, each for the other, on separate occasions, but hold back on declaring their feelings until they are nearly wrenched from each other permanently. For what reasons did they hold back? Have you ever resisted loving someone? What kind of love is this that can contain reservations—human love or God's kind of love? Does God ever have reservations about loving us?

11. Maddie struggles to trust God, other people and even herself because of the tragedies in her background and the missing pieces of her memory. However, the loneliness of this self-imposed emotional isolation eventually becomes unbearable. What aspect of her conversation in the garden with David Greene finally breaks through her wall of distrust? Why?

12. The temptation to take David up on his offer of escape is compelling to both Maddie and Chris. Why? What is the fatal flaw in their individual reasons to accept

David's offer? Is it ever right to act against your conscience to protect someone else?

13. Why was the governor's announcement about the cartel's annihilation a bittersweet moment for Maddie? How would you reassure her that her comrades in arms did not die in vain, despite the failure of their mission? Can you apply this reassurance to others in the military who have lost fellow soldiers to operations that met with disaster?

REQUEST YOUR FREE BOOKS!

2 FREE RIVETING INSPIRATIONAL NOVELS
PLUS 2 FREE MYSTERY GIFTS

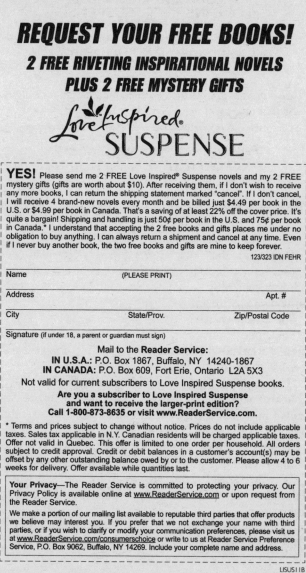

Love Inspired®
SUSPENSE

YES! Please send me 2 FREE Love Inspired® Suspense novels and my 2 FREE mystery gifts (gifts are worth about $10). After receiving them, if I don't wish to receive any more books, I can return the shipping statement marked "cancel". If I don't cancel, I will receive 4 brand-new novels every month and be billed just $4.49 per book in the U.S. or $4.99 per book in Canada. That's a saving of at least 22% off the cover price. It's quite a bargain! Shipping and handling is just 50¢ per book in the U.S. and 75¢ per book in Canada.* I understand that accepting the 2 free books and gifts places me under no obligation to buy anything. I can always return a shipment and cancel at any time. Even if I never buy another book, the two free books and gifts are mine to keep forever.

123/323 IDN FEHR

Name	(PLEASE PRINT)	
Address		Apt. #
City	State/Prov.	Zip/Postal Code

Signature (if under 18, a parent or guardian must sign)

Mail to the **Reader Service:**
IN U.S.A.: P.O. Box 1867, Buffalo, NY 14240-1867
IN CANADA: P.O. Box 609, Fort Erie, Ontario L2A 5X3

Not valid for current subscribers to Love Inspired Suspense books.

**Are you a subscriber to Love Inspired Suspense
and want to receive the larger-print edition?
Call 1-800-873-8635 or visit www.ReaderService.com.**

* Terms and prices subject to change without notice. Prices do not include applicable taxes. Sales tax applicable in N.Y. Canadian residents will be charged applicable taxes. Offer not valid in Quebec. This offer is limited to one order per household. All orders subject to credit approval. Credit or debit balances in a customer's account(s) may be offset by any other outstanding balance owed by or to the customer. Please allow 4 to 6 weeks for delivery. Offer available while quantities last.

Your Privacy—The Reader Service is committed to protecting your privacy. Our Privacy Policy is available online at www.ReaderService.com or upon request from the Reader Service.

We make a portion of our mailing list available to reputable third parties that offer products we believe may interest you. If you prefer that we not exchange your name with third parties, or if you wish to clarify or modify your communication preferences, please visit us at www.ReaderService.com/consumerschoice or write to us at Reader Service Preference Service, P.O. Box 9062, Buffalo, NY 14269. Include your complete name and address.

LISUS11B

Brave police officers tackle crime with the help of their canine partners in TEXAS K-9 UNIT, *an exciting new series from Love Inspired® Suspense.*

Read on for a preview of the first book,
TRACKING JUSTICE by Shirlee McCoy.

Police detective Austin Black glanced at his dashboard clock as he raced up Oak Drive. Two in the morning. Not a good time to get a call about a missing child.

Then again, there was never a good time for that; never a good time to look in the worried eyes of a parent or to follow a scent trail and know that it might lead to a joyful reunion or a sorrowful goodbye.

If it led anywhere.

Sometimes trails went cold, scents were lost and the missing were never found. Austin wanted to bring them all home safe. Hopefully, this time, he would.

He pulled into the driveway of a small house.

Justice whined. A three-year-old bloodhound, he was trained in search and rescue and knew when it was time to work.

Austin jumped out of the vehicle when a woman darted out the front door. "You called about a missing child?"

"Yes. My son. I heard Brady call for me, and when I walked into his room, he was gone." She ran back up the porch stairs.

Austin jogged in after her. She waved from a doorway. "This is my son's room."

Austin followed her into the room. "How old is your son, Ms....?"

"Billows. Eva. He's seven."

"Did you argue?"

"We didn't argue about anything, Officer..."

"Detective Austin Black. I'm with Sagebrush Police Department's Special Operation K-9 Unit."

"You have a search dog with you?" Her face brightened. "I can give you something of his. A shirt or—"

"Hold on. I need to get a little more information first."

"How about you start out there?" She gestured to the window.

"Was it open when you came in the room?"

"Yes. It looks like someone carried Brady out the window. But I don't know how anyone could have gotten into his room when all the doors and windows were locked."

"You're sure?"

"Of course." She frowned. "I always double-check. I have ever since..."

"What?"

"Nothing that matters. I just need to find my son."

Hiding something?

"Everything matters when a child is missing, Eva."

To see Justice the bloodhound in action, pick up
TRACKING JUSTICE by Shirlee McCoy.
Available January 2013 from Love Inspired® Suspense.

SHLISEXP1212

Love Inspired®
SUSPENSE
RIVETING INSPIRATIONAL ROMANCE

TEXAS K-9 UNIT

Lawmen that solve the toughest cases with the help of their brave canine partners.

Follow Lone Star State police officers and their canine partners in action each month as they get closer to not only uncovering a mastermind criminal but also finding love.

Available wherever books are sold.

www.LoveInspiredBooks.com

LISCONT13R